Sweet revenge?

Tess sat down, then noticed the balloon on the stool at the end of the counter. On second glance, she realized it wasn't a balloon at all, but a giant doll. A giant, naked doll. Bewildered, she looked over at Drew. But he made no move to explain the third member of their dinner party. In truth, he acted as if they were still…alone.

Finally, Tess could stand it no longer. "Who's the other woman?" she asked. "Old girlfriend?"

"A gift. She was delivered to my office late this afternoon, along with some other interesting items." He shoved a small box in her direction. "Open it."

Tess stared at the box and silently cursed her sister. Then she reached inside and withdrew a pair of bikini underpants made of a strange, sticky fabric.

"Edible," Drew said. "I thought we'd save them for dessert. I have a bottle of port that would complement them nicely."

A giggle slipped from Tess's lips as she tossed the underwear back in the box. "You seem to be taking this rather well," she ventured.

"Do I? Looks can be deceiving." He paused, meeting her eyes. "You're a creative person, Tess. Maybe you could help me plan a little payback?" At her questioning look, he added, "It's time I got my revenge."

Dear Reader,

I have some very exciting news! In May of this year, we are launching a great new series called Harlequin Duets.

Harlequin Duets will offer two brand-new novels in one book for one low price. You will continue enjoying wonderful romantic comedy-type stories from more of the authors you've come to love! The two Harlequin Duets novels to be published every month will each contain two stories, creating four wonderful reading experiences each month. We're bringing you twice as much fun and romance with Harlequin Duets!

Longtime fan favorite Julie Kistler joins the Harlequin Love & Laughter line-up with *50 WAYS TO LURE YOUR LOVER*. Set in the offices of the fictional *Real Men* magazine (you'll find more of these stories in months to come), reporter Mabel Ivey finds herself the subject of a glamorous makeover and learns all about life as a sex object. She has to admit it's fun, but when the man of her dreams starts pursuing her, she's not sure if he's in love with the *new* her or the *real* her. Popular Temptation author Kate Hoffmann also makes her debut into the Love & Laughter series with *SWEET REVENGE?* The heroine, Tess Ryan, is in a bit of a fix. Her sister is hell-bent on getting revenge—on the man Tess has fallen in love with. Have fun watching revenge run amok in the most hilarious ways.

This is the last month you will find Love & Laughter on sale. I'd like to thank you for enjoying these stories—we, the editors, loved working on them. Don't forget to look for Harlequin Duets, on sale later this month!

Humorously yours,

Malle Vallik

Malle Vallik
Associate Senior Editor

SWEET REVENGE?
Kate Hoffmann

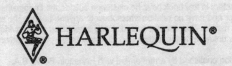

HARLEQUIN®

TORONTO • NEW YORK • LONDON
AMSTERDAM • PARIS • SYDNEY • HAMBURG
STOCKHOLM • ATHENS • TOKYO • MILAN • MADRID
PRAGUE • WARSAW • BUDAPEST • AUCKLAND

ISBN 0-373-44066-9

SWEET REVENGE?

Copyright © 1999 by Peggy Hoffmann

A Note from the Author

A girl has to kiss a lot of frogs before she finds her prince. And sometimes, she's got to kiss a few weasels, snakes and worms, too!

The point is, real-life relationships don't always end up happily ever after. The idea behind *Sweet Revenge?* came from, of all places, a talk show. The day I tuned in, one of the guests was a young woman who ran a revenge business. Every day, she got even with a few of those charming men (we've all met them), who have done us women wrong. This got me thinking...and when I get thinking, I usually find a book in there somewhere.

So the subject is revenge—and in this case, revenge run amok. I hope you enjoy Tess's misadventures along the road to finding her very own prince. If you enjoy this book, make sure to look for my other books in the Harlequin Temptation series, including *Not In My Bed!*, available next month.

Happy Reading,

Kate Hoffmann

Kate Hoffmann

To the memory of LuAnn Fieber Demler,
a friend who loved to laugh.

1

"LUCY? Come on, sweetie. Come out from under the bed."

Tess Ryan bent down and peered beneath the dust ruffle into the darkness. Though she couldn't see Lucy, she could hear her soft snuffling and slow, even breathing. She held out the bowl of ice cream, hoping to lure Lucy from her hiding place. Ice cream always did the trick.

The house had been dark when Tess arrived home from work. Lucy was usually there to greet her, but tonight, when Tess walked in, she'd been met with silence. She'd kicked off her shoes and begun the search, ending up on the floor next to the high four-poster bed in her bedroom.

"You don't have to hide," she murmured in a soothing voice. "Come on, honey. Come on out. We'll have ice cream. We'll lie on the bed and watch some television. I'll brush your hair."

Whenever Lucy was scared or upset, she retreated to that dark underworld usually reserved for dust bunnies, dirty socks and discarded magazines. And had Lucy been a dog or a cat, perhaps Tess might not have been so perturbed. But Lucy was Tess's little sister—her twenty-nine-year-old little sister, to be perfectly precise—and Tess had come to the conclusion that retreating beneath the bed was a childhood habit that needed to be broken once and for all.

"This is ridiculous," Tess said, pushing up to her feet.

A muffled voice rose from beneath the bed. "It's nice to know that my only sister thinks my problems are ridiculous."

Tess flopped down on the bed and kicked her feet up, flexing her toes and sighing softly. "I don't think your problems are ridiculous, Luce. I think the way you deal with them is ridiculous."

"If it makes me feel better, then Dr. Standish says it's all right!" Lucy cried.

"I wonder if Dr. Standish would say the same if you were hiding under *his* bed," Tess muttered. She waited for a reply, but there was none. "I'm not going to speak to you until you come out. I'm covering my ears now. Don't bother talking."

Tess plucked the spoon from the bowl and began to savor the ice cream that she'd used to entice her sister. The rich vanilla slid down her throat and brought a smile to her lips. When she finished, she wiped the last creamy bits from the bowl with her finger then reached for a magazine from the bedside table.

She'd had a long day and an even longer evening. The last thing she wanted was to end it all with one of Lucy's epic emotional scenes. Maybe if she just stayed quiet, her sister would fall asleep and Tess wouldn't have to deal with her. But that hope was short-lived when Tess heard a sob from beneath the box spring.

"You could be more supportive," Lucy called.

"Was that talking? I can't hear a thing," Tess reminded her. "If you want to discuss the events of your day, we'll do it like grown-ups or not at all."

Her sister, Lucy Ryan Courault Battenfield Oleska, had moved back home to Atlanta two years ago, right after she'd divorced her third husband, the Romanian soccer player, and right before she started dating the British banker. Tess had been living at their family home in Buckhead while looking for a house to buy. But when their father decided to take a new post in the diplomatic corps and moved with his second wife to Warsaw, Tess and Lucy inherited the care of the huge family mansion for an indefinite period of time. Free rent far outweighed the liabilities of living with Lucy, and Tess had jumped at the chance.

It didn't take Lucy long to fall back into old childhood habits—taking naps in the middle of the flower beds that encircled the backyard, crawling out the nursery window on the third floor to perch on the slate roof and hiding beneath the bed whenever her emotional state reached a crisis.

Lucy was what most people would call eccentric. But Tess knew better. Her sister was willful and spoiled and had been indulged her entire life. After their mother died, Tess's father had done everything he could to ease the loss. While Tess had become stronger and more independent, Lucy had become needy and clinging, always relying on Tess to smooth out all her troubles, then latching on to a series of unsuitable husbands.

As a fifteen-year-old, Tess didn't mind the added responsibilities. Protecting and sheltering Lucy was what her mother would have wanted. And her father, distant in his grief, wasn't prepared to raise two young girls. They were as close as sisters could be, Lucy depending on Tess for nurturing and Tess depending on Lucy for affection and admiration.

But as adults, they couldn't have been more different than caviar and cottage cheese. Lucy Ryan lived a Technicolor life, always poised on the edge of emotional upheaval, drifting toward unsuitable suitors and romantic disasters like a bee to honey. Lucy loved being in love.

Unfortunately, she changed boyfriends about as often as Tess took out the garbage—a connection that spoke more for Tess's housekeeping abilities than for Lucy's companions.

"You are so mean!" Lucy cried, giving the underside of the bed a kick.

"Yes, I am!" Tess countered. "I'm a hateful person. I don't know how you stand to live with me!"

A ragged wail echoed from her sister's hiding place and Tess winced, knowing exactly what lay ahead. A long night of commiserating and cajoling, of attempts to assure her sister that the man she'd just lost wasn't worth having in the first place. This had all become such a regular part of their life together that Tess was sure she could get a job as a therapist if her party-planning business ever went bust.

There wasn't much chance of that, she mused. She'd built a successful business planning special events—wonderful corporate parties and sparkling galas for nonprofits all over the metropolitan area. Tess was a natural organizer. As a teenager, she'd engineered elaborate dinner parties for her father, affairs for forty where she served as hostess until her stepmother had come along.

She'd even been profiled in a recent magazine article as Atlanta's newest "party girl," publicity that had brought in even more business. But contrary to her professional image, Tess was far from a die-hard "party girl." She preferred to spend her evenings on the sidelines, in the shadows, watching her creative vision and precise organization blossom into an unforgettable event, taking satisfaction in a happy clientele. She became the quintessential wallflower at her own party, draped in a dress that she'd be more than willing to trade for a pair of jeans and an old sweatshirt.

Tess closed her eyes and listened to Lucy's dramatic weeping. It was only Thursday night and she had three other parties scheduled for the weekend—a fund-raiser at the art museum on Friday night, a political dinner and dance on Saturday evening and a lavish fiftieth birthday party for one of Atlanta's most prominent businessmen on Sunday. And dealing with Lucy's latest crisis would take more energy than all three parties put together.

Tess pushed up off the bed. "I'm going to get a glass of wine," she called as she walked out of the bedroom. "Do you want anything?"

"Cheese doodles!" Lucy replied. "And peanut butter...a bottle of scotch...and bring those double-stuffed Oreos along."

Tess wandered down the hall, passing Lucy's room on the way. She pushed the door open and flipped on the light, then shook her head. "This is worse than I thought," she murmured, surveying the carnage, shards of shattered porcelain on the hardwood floor. Her sister collected Hummels, romantically sweet figurines of little girls and little boys, that she displayed throughout her room. "A five-Hummel breakup." Lucy's previous record had been three.

By the time Tess returned to her room carrying a tray of food, her sister had crawled up onto the bed. She was wearing her most tattered flannel nightgown. Her eyes and nose were red, her dark hair tangled, her usually impeccable makeup smudged. "The human race would be better off without men!" Lucy cried dramatically.

Tess crossed the room and set the tray down on the bedside table, then pulled a wad of tissue from the box on Lucy's lap. She held them beneath her sister's nose. "Luce, without men, there would be no human race. Females need males to procreate. You're here due to the efforts of the opposite sex.''

Lucy blew her nose and tossed the tissue over her shoulder. ''Well, the next time I see Daddy, I'll thank him for the favor.''

With an impatient sigh, Tess bent down and began to pluck the used tissues from the floor. ''So, are you going to tell me what happened? Or are you just going to trash my room?''

''We should get rid of all the men,'' Lucy said, her arms flying out for emphasis. ''So what if we couldn't procreate? The sex isn't *that* great. And we'd all be so happy...'' Her lower lip trembled and a fresh trail of tears dribbled down her cheeks. ''Did I ever tell you about his eyes? He had the most beautiful brown eyes. And a little cleft in his chin. And...and...sweet, little...apple cheeks.'' A miserable wail burst from her throat and Lucy threw herself onto the bed, burying her face in Tess's pillow.

Tess stared at her sister, grabbed a tissue, tore it apart and stuffed a bit in both ears. The crying jag would probably go on for the rest of the night and into the next day. At the rate they were going, Tess could expect her sister to run out of tears sometime next month, about the time she met her newest man.

Tess reached for the bag of cheese doodles, and popped a handful into her mouth. How could they be sisters and be so different? Tess was rational and focused. Lucy was emotional and spontaneous. Tess hadn't had a date in almost two years. In that same amount of time, Lucy had managed at least four major relationships and a score of minor flings. And with each man came the inevitable breakup, the biblical flood of tears and the vows to enter the first convent she found with figure-flattering habits and a lenient hair policy.

Tess should have seen this coming. But she had thought that this man—this Andy Wyatt, the famous architect—was different. Sure, Lucy had only been dating him for two months, but this was serious dating. He'd taken her to all the best restaurants in Atlanta. They'd spent a long week in Maui and last weekend in San Francisco. Tess had even asked for a few details about the man, although she knew by now not to become too invested in Lucy's love life.

According to Lucy, this man had a gorgeous house in Dunwoody, a fancy car and money to burn. He made his living as the architect of choice in certain tony Atlanta circles but he was a very private person. Tess needn't have asked for more. She knew Lucy's taste in men. He'd be breathtakingly handsome, suave and sophisticated, a man who made women swoon and stutter and stumble over each other to gain his attention. As for "private," that was just a nice word for arrogant.

"Luce, he isn't worth it. He's just another one of those guys…"

Another one of those successful men that Lucy always had at hand and Tess could never seem to find. It wasn't as if Tess didn't meet men. Her parties were teaming with eligible members of the opposite sex. But unlike Lucy, she could never find the right words, the subtle approach, the winning combination of a good hair day and a dress that didn't make her look like the "before" picture in a weight-loss ad.

"I—I just wish you could have met him," Lucy murmured, her voice muffled by the pillow. "Andy was so cute."

"It's probably better I didn't meet him, Luce. This way I can't hunt him down and kill him for the dog he is."

This brought a soft giggle from Lucy. She pushed up and smiled at her sister. "He is a low-down dog. He led me on. He made me promises. He even told me that he loved me. And then, he just dumped me!" A fresh flood of tears pushed at the corners of her eyes and Tess caught the first spill with a tissue.

"Here's what we're going to do," Tess said. "First, I want you to sit up and stop crying."

Lucy did as she was told, wiping her damp cheeks with her fingertips. "I'm not going to do that list thing again," she warned. "You made me do that with Raoul. I don't believe in all that self-help mumbo jumbo."

Why would she? Lucy led with her heart and Tess with her head. While Tess spent her weekends reading books on spiritual wellness and emotional improvement, Lucy threw herself, full tilt, into life and love. Tess could only hope that her sister would learn to take a more prudent approach when it came to men. "That self-help mumbo jumbo helped you get over Raoul, didn't it? You came up with five things he did that drove you nuts."

"And I'm not doing that visualization exercise either. There's no way I can imagine Andy as a toad. Or a cockroach. Or a snake."

"I have a better idea," Tess said. She grabbed a book from the bedside table. "Closure," she said, flipping through the pages. "It's an actual psychological theory. You have to do something to put a proper end to your relationship."

"I could call him," Lucy said, her eyes brightening. "Maybe if he knew how distraught I was, he'd see his mistake. He'd see that he shouldn't have dumped me like he did."

"Closure means putting an end to everything, not start-ing it all over again!" Tess cried.

"Well, how am I supposed to let him know I know it's over if I can't call him and tell him it's over?"

"It only has to be over in your mind. This is a symbolic end. Like burning everything he gave you. That would be closure."

Lucy sighed, her shoulders drooping. She methodically shredded a tissue as she spoke. "But he gave me some really nice stuff," she whined. "Why would I want to burn it?"

Tess sighed. "All right. So we won't burn your stuff. But we can plan an appropriate little punctuation for this man in your life. A fitting end."

"What I'd really like to burn is that fancy house. Or—or I could drive his precious car right into his swimming pool. Or dye his damn dog green!"

"You can't do something criminal," Tess explained.

"Dying his dog green would not be criminal. It would be an improvement. That dog is as ugly as a mud fence."

"Luce, you broke up with him, not the dog. Leave the poor pooch out of this."

"Then you think of something," Lucy said with a pout. "You're the planner in the family. And you're much more creative than me."

"I can't plan your closure for you. It doesn't work that way."

"Yes, you can. I trust you."

Tess considered the notion for a moment, weighing the request against her need for sleep. She sighed softly. "All right. If I do it, you have to stop crying. And you have to get out of my room and let me go to sleep. We'll discuss it tomorrow evening after I get home and we'll come up with an appropriate plan."

Lucy's expression brightened. "What are you going to do to him? Will it hurt? It should be at least a little painful."

"I don't know what we'll do," Tess said. "I'll think of something."

TESS STOOD in a corner of the bustling kitchen and chewed on her fingernail. Waiters in bow ties and pleated shirts hustled back and forth to the reception area, leaving with trays filled with delectable hors d'oeuvres and returning with empty champagne flutes. The catering staff, in white coats and toques, shouted between themselves, efficiently and artfully arranging a delicious array of nibbles for the cocktail crowd at the art museum fund-raiser.

Everything was going as well as could be expected, except for an unorganized wait staff. She had attempted to bring some type of order and discipline to the chaos, but the manager of the wait staff had mysteriously disappeared before she'd had the chance to speak to him. The caterers were loath to give the unfamiliar waiters any criticism for fear their food would be left to grow cold in retaliation and the waiters weren't interested in her suggestions.

"Double booking," Tess muttered. The scourge of the party-planning industry. She should have known better than to try out a new crew of waiters on such an important party. But her regular guys had been booked for a big business reception downtown and she'd always tried to cultivate new sources.

As she searched the kitchen for a waiter who looked open to constructive criticism, her gaze stopped at a tall, slender man moving along the stainless-steel counter, plucking hors d'oeuvres from filled silver trays and popping them into his mouth. Ah, the manager of the wait staff. Tess narrowed her eyes and stalked across the kitchen, her temper rising with each step.

"It's about time you got here!" she cried, grabbing the jacket from his arm and shoving a tray into his hands. "I asked for twenty waiters and you sent sixteen. I asked for supervisory personnel and you disappear for—"

She glanced up at his face and the admonishment died in her throat. Deep blue eyes twinkled and a lazy smile curled his finely chiseled mouth. "Three hours," she murmured, her voice cracking. Tess had met a lot of waiters in her day, but she'd never met one quite as…gorgeous. And the way he looked at her, with a mixture of devastating charm and barely suppressed humor. When all the while he ought to be looking contrite and apologetic.

"What's your name?" she snapped, scolding herself silently. Drooling over the waiters was not allowed! This man worked for her and his irresponsibility was reflecting badly on her reputation.

"My friends call me Drew. And what's your name, ma'am?"

His voice was so deep and rich, she managed to ignore his impertinence and forced a tight smile. "Well, Mr. Drew, if you had any business acumen you'd know that I'm the woman who hired you. And I'll be the woman who'll make your life a living hell if you don't get out there and direct your wait staff. They're not circulating with fresh champagne, they're moving way too slow with the hot hors d'oeuvres and there are dirty little plates and napkins scattered all over the room. Now, get out there and do your job!"

Tess shoved a tray of crab claws into his hands, turned him around and pushed him toward the swinging doors. He shot a bemused look over his shoulder, then shrugged and grinned. "I love a woman who knows what she wants."

"Now, maybe I can relax a little," she murmured, tossing his jacket on the counter.

But her respite lasted all of three minutes, coming to an abrupt end when Marceline Lavery burst through the kitchen door, all bugle beads and diamonds and beauty-pageant hair. Marceline, a former Miss Georgia, was the president of the art museum's board of directors and the host of the evening's event. When she saw Tess, she waved her jewel-laden arms and swept over, her designer gown swirling around her feet. "Ms. Ryan! A moment of your time, please."

Tess hurried toward her, concerned at the imperious tone of Marceline's voice. Marceline was one of her oldest and best clients. Tess had planned charity events for nearly every organization that Mrs. Lavery worked for, along with many personal parties at the Lavery mansion on Paces Ferry Road. She even coordinated the annual Lavery barbecue, one of Atlanta's biggest social events of the summer season.

"Is there a problem?"

Marceline cleared her throat. "There is a member of our board of directors out there passing around a tray of crab claws. He told me you ordered him to get to work."

Tess touched her fingers to her lips and blinked in shock. "Oh, Mrs. Lavery, I'm so sorry. I thought he was..." She smoothed her skirt and smiled apologetically, then grabbed the man's jacket from the counter. "I—I'll take care of it, Mrs. Lavery. Right away. Please, accept my apologies."

With that, Tess spun on her heel and raced out of the kitchen. Weaving through the crowd, she searched for the handsome man with the dark hair, the intriguing blue eyes...and the tray of crab claws. She spotted him near the ice sculpture, still holding the tray and chatting with an attractive blonde.

"I'll take that, sir," she said, sidling up beside him. She snatched the tray from his grasp and handed him his coat. Hoping to make a graceful exit, Tess turned and rushed back toward the kitchen. But to her utter mortification, he deserted the blonde and followed hard on her heels as she navigated through the crowd. "You can stop following me," she muttered, risking a glance over her shoulder. "Your short career as a waiter is over."

He chuckled, a warm, easy sound that made Tess's embarrassment even more acute. Rather than being insulted, he had the good manners to appear amused. "And I was just getting the hang of passing that tray around," he said. "I was looking forward to trying a tray of champagne."

Tess turned to him when she reached the kitchen door. "You could have told me who you were," she said, her gaze fixed on the crab claws. She methodically rearranged them on the tray, then looked up.

He grinned. "And spoil my fun?"

"What were you doing in the kitchen in the first place?" Tess demanded.

His gaze skimmed over her face like a soft caress, pausing briefly on her mouth before moving on. "I was hungry. I'd been on a plane for thirteen hours and I wanted something to eat that didn't taste like it had been made two days ago. Besides, there's never any time to eat at these events. Everyone wants to talk." He grabbed a glass of champagne from a passing waiter and took a sip, then sighed. "God, I hate these parties. They are so deadly dull."

Tess swallowed hard and pasted a benign smile on her face. "Do you hate *this* party?"

He took another swallow of his drink and surveyed the room indifferently. "As a rule, I hate all parties."

"Good," she murmured, a warm blush flooding her cheeks. "For a moment there, I was deeply insulted. Now I'm just slightly disparaged."

He looked over at her, his eyebrow quirked up in question.

"I planned this entire party," she explained. "From the food to the decorations." Tess balanced the tray on her hip and held out her hand. "Tess Ryan. Parties Perfect."

"Tess," he repeated. "I should have known. Well, it's nice to meet you, Tess. If you'll just give me a moment, I'll pull my foot out of my mouth and we can start over again."

Tess laughed at his rueful dismay. Even embarrassment seemed utterly charming on this man. "Was that an apology, Mr. Drew?"

"It's just Drew," he said, leaning close. "Besides, if we're on a first-name basis, Tess, maybe you'll forgive me for the insult. To tell the truth, I've had a sudden change of heart regarding this party. I think it's wonderful. The best ever. A first-rate barn burner."

"I'll forgive you only if you forgive *me* for shoving that tray into your hands."

"Deal," Drew said, taking her hand and giving it a firm shake. "Now, why don't you and I get out of here and find a quiet place where I can insult you and you can berate me in private."

Tess giggled. For a moment, she thought he might be serious, but then realized that this was just part of his teasing. He really was too charming for his own good— and hers. "I'm working. I can't leave."

"I'll explain to the powers that be," he insisted, glancing in Mrs. Lavery's direction.

"You *are* the powers that be," Tess replied. "Mrs. Lavery said you were a member of the board of directors. Are you famous?" she asked, her eyebrow arching dubiously. "Or are you just filthy rich? You have to be one or the other. Unless, of course, you're a direct descendant of Robert E. Lee or Jefferson Davis, which makes you royalty."

He drank the last of his champagne. "None of the above. I'm just a guy who likes fine art. And I look good in a tux."

Tess sighed. He certainly did. She used to believe that any man would look good in black tie, but Drew had changed that opinion. Now she truly believed that the tuxedo had been designed especially with him in mind—his broad shoulders, his narrow waist and deeply tanned features. Even the careless cut of his hair made an arresting contrast to the stark formality of his dress.

"How about just one dance?" he said.

Was he serious? Did he actually expect her to walk onto the dance floor in front of all these people and...dance? After all, this man couldn't possibly find *her* attractive. She attracted men with severe psychological problems...or men who had a wife stashed in the suburbs...or men who dressed in ladies' underwear. Her sister, Lucy, attracted men like Drew.

"Thank you, but I've been embarrassed enough," Tess said. She wasn't much of a dancer, though any woman would probably look good in this man's arms. Her blood warmed as she imagined him touching her, sliding his hand around her waist, splaying his fingers across her back, standing so close that her hips brushed his. She moaned softly.

"Is that a yes?" he asked.

Shaken out of her fantasy, Tess glanced up at him and

smiled wanly. "I'm afraid I can't. I'm working. It just wouldn't be right for the hired help to enjoy the party along with the guests."

"Well, I'm not going to take no for an answer," Drew replied. "If we can't dance here, we'll find a place more befitting your station." He grabbed her hand and tugged her along behind him, through the kitchen doors, past the caterers and the security guard watching the service entrance, and into the alley behind the art museum.

He stopped in front of a Dumpster and pulled her into his arms, then began to hum an off-key tune. "Better?" he asked.

Tess surveyed their surroundings. "The ambience is certainly a change." She sniffed. "And the smell...well, it could be worse." In truth, the setting couldn't be more disgusting, the odor of garbage wafting through the air, scraps of paper blowing beneath their feet, the catering truck belching exhaust. Yet it felt so incredibly romantic with this man.

"You're the first girl I've ever brought here," he teased, his breath warm against her ear. "I wanted you to know that."

"I'm touched," she replied in the same lighthearted tone. "Most men take me to fancy restaurants and chic nightclubs. But you..."

"I have a broom closet I'd like to show you after we get to know each other a little better."

They danced in the alley for a long time, neither one of them saying a word, their silly mood replaced with a current of attraction that even Tess couldn't rationalize or ignore. A magic mood descended around them and she forgot about the smell of garbage and the audience of rodents that were probably watching them from the shadows. Instead, she focused on the man who held her in his arms.

Tess had never really believed in love at first sight. She'd never been immediately attracted to a man—until this very moment. And she didn't even know his last name. Resting her cheek on his shoulder, she sighed softly. Did she really care? All she wanted was to spend the rest of the night in his arms. She'd worry about proprieties and formalities later.

Her mind flashed to Lucy, to the myriad problems that overwhelming attraction caused. After all, what did Tess know about this man, besides the fact that he served on the museum's board of directors? He could be a socially prominent psychopath. Considering her luck in the love department, that wouldn't be so far-fetched. But for now, she wanted to believe that he was a handsome and charming and intelligent man who found her as attractive as she found him.

"I almost didn't come to this party," he murmured. "I'm glad I did."

Tess pushed back and looked up at him. "I'm not sure if you're teasing or if you're being serious."

He stopped dancing and his gazed locked with hers. "I'm serious," he said, bending closer. "Very serious."

She knew he was going to kiss her and Tess wanted to let the moment spin out in front of them until their lips met. But reason took over and she stiffened. This was all happening way too fast! It was all too...Lucyesque. Too dangerous, too irrational. If she'd learned anything as Lucy Ryan's sister, it was never to trust the motives of men, especially handsome, wealthy, charming men. She drew a deep breath and tried to cover her apprehension. She couldn't let him kiss her. She barely knew him!

"I—I really have to get back to work," she stammered,

pulling out of his arms. "Thanks for being so understanding."

"Understanding?"

"About the crab claws," she said. "Maybe we'll run into each other again. I plan a lot of these parties…and I guess you go to a lot of these parties. The odds are good that—"

"Oh, we'll see each other again, Tess Ryan," he said, reaching out to brush his fingers along her arm. "You can bet on that."

Tess felt a flush rise in her cheeks as she backed away. Lord, he was sexy. And devilishly good-looking. And if she wasn't mistaken, he was doing his very best to charm her into staying in the alley. And she was making a complete mess of this! "I—I don't gamble," she said softly as she backed toward the door.

"You should," he said, crossing his arms over his chest, "especially if you're betting on a sure thing."

By the time she reached the safety of the kitchen, Tess had already decided that she'd mistaken his attention for genuine interest. He was a profligate flirt and he'd probably charmed scores of beautiful women. She'd just been a way to pass time at a dull party, to offer some relief from social chitchat.

She grabbed a cheese straw from a passing tray and munched on it thoughtfully. She'd been right to trust her instincts. He'd merely been toying with her, leading her on. No doubt if she'd allowed herself, they would have left the party, headed to some hotel room and made mad, passionate love, just like Lucy would have. And then he would have disappeared from her life, never to be heard from again.

Tess sighed. She'd listened to so many of Lucy's horror stories that she'd become jaded and cynical. Still, it wasn't hard to see why Lucy had the problems she did. Resisting a handsome and charming man was much more difficult than Tess could have imagined, especially when she wanted to throw herself into his arms and let human nature take its course.

"Maybe it's time to cut Lucy some slack," she murmured to herself.

2

Andrew Wyatt braced his shoulder against the Dumpster outside the service entrance to the art museum, staring into the dark alley. He had found a spot upwind and waited. The reception had ended almost an hour before and he'd been assured by a friendly security guard that all those remaining inside would be required to leave through the rear entrance.

She couldn't have slipped out before him, he thought. He'd spent the remainder of the reception keeping a surreptitious but intrigued eye out for Tess Ryan. Every now and then she'd appear in the crowd to check on the food or consult the musicians before she disappeared again into the kitchen. She'd always take a long look around and he imagined that she was looking for him, though in reality, she was probably just doing her job.

Lord, she was pretty. He'd dated his share of beautiful women, but they paled in comparison to Tess Ryan. Everything about her was uncomplicated, from the practical style of her dark hair to the simple cut of her black cocktail dress. And he needed an uncomplicated woman, now that he'd made the decision that he needed a woman in his life at all.

Drew had never been much for long-term relationships, but lately he'd found his life lacking when it came to love. He had traveled all over the world, working on new and exciting design projects, enjoying a career as an architect that most men could only dream about. But when he came home, he opened the door to an empty house, a house that seemed to grow more cold and lonely with every passing day. And he found himself envying those men with their wives and their families and their dinner-table conversation. He'd considered his options on the flight back from Tokyo, and had made a resolution as he walked in the front door after nearly two months away.

The change had been a long time in coming. He had made his first step toward commitment a year ago by buying an aquarium and stocking it with tropical fish. Drew had hoped that a few fish might make his house seem more like a home. But fish didn't offer much in the way of companionship or conversation. To be honest, they barely noticed he was alive.

So, he decided to try a dog. Man's best friend, a canine companion to share his home. He'd chosen the ugliest dog in the pound, hoping that a mutt with so little to recommend itself would be more appreciative and feel obligated to enjoy his company. But Rufus had preferred the company of the fish, spending most of his free time staring at the aquarium. And when Drew gave the fish away to a friend, Rufus turned to television, parking himself in front of the tube for most of his waking hours.

The only human—beyond the stars of daytime television—that Rufus related to was Elliot Cosgrove, Drew's business manager. Elliot watched Drew's house when he was out of town, watered the plants, supervised the housekeeper and gardener and kept an eye on Rufus. They seemed to share a secret bond, Elliot and Rufus, a relationship that Drew couldn't comprehend. He could only speculate that they saw a little of themselves in each other—a painfully shy man and an orphan dog.

If Drew hadn't been so determined to win over Rufus,

he would have given him to Elliot. After all, they probably belonged together. But he wasn't ready to admit that he couldn't make a committed relationship work, even if it was with a dog. He needed some continuity in his life, someone or something he could depend on. And if he couldn't get Rufus to love him, how was he supposed to get a woman to commit?

Everyone expected him to marry into one of Atlanta's moneyed families. But even though he moved in wealthy circles, it was only for business purposes. He found little in common with his clients, and the only thing that really set him apart was his talent for architectural design. After all, he was the son of a Seattle construction worker and a math teacher, not some blue-blooded descendant of a Civil War hero. He had more in common with the security guard watching the door than with Marceline Lavery and her crowd.

His friendship with Mrs. Lavery had been good for one thing, Drew mused. He'd gotten Tess Ryan's phone number along with a rundown of her professional credentials, marking the very first time anything good had come of attending one of these social functions. If all else failed, he knew he could call Tess Ryan in a few weeks with some story about planning a reception for his firm. Or maybe an anniversary party for his parents, even though his parents lived in Seattle. He could spend a few hours on the phone talking to her, take a few meetings with her then casually ask her out to lunch.

"Or you could cut right to the chase and invite her out for a drink this very night," he muttered to himself. Considering his complete lack of a social life lately, and his recent resolution, he had decided to wait for her in the alley and try his luck. He wasn't exactly desperate. But when a woman as pretty and smart as Tess Ryan stumbled into his life, he couldn't just let her walk out. Besides, how could she refuse?

Drew Wyatt was known in some circles as one of Atlanta's most eligible bachelors, though he'd done absolutely nothing to perpetuate that image. He shunned publicity at every turn and refused invitations that were so obviously setups. Still, he managed to meet an endless string of beautiful women looking for a wealthy and prominent husband.

But he'd never gotten past a second date with most of them. In all honesty, he hadn't had a *first* date in almost six months. Now that he was back home for an extended period of time, he was ready. His life was about to take a turn for the better and Tess Ryan was the woman to make it happen.

Drew heard the sound of high heels on the concrete walk. He waited in the shadows of the Dumpster, reconsidering his plan, until she was just a few feet away. "You should have taken the bet, Ms. Ryan," he said.

She jumped at his voice and stared in his direction, her pretty green eyes wide. Her surprise gradually gave way to a hesitant smile as he emerged from the darkness. "I told you we'd see each other again."

"If I would have known you were hanging around," she said with a coy smile, "I would have put you to work cleaning up. You're great with a tray."

"I thought I'd walk you to your car," Drew said. "And on the way, I'd try to convince you to have a cup of coffee with me."

She looked at him, an odd expression on her face, disbelief mixed with pleasure and tinged with apprehension. "You're asking me to have coffee? Now? Tonight?"

"Are you busy? Do you have other plans?" Drew

cursed softly. "I'm sorry. You're probably tired and I shouldn't have presumed that you would just—"

"No!" Tess said. "I'm just surprised. I mean, I don't go out much, and with my job, it's hard to meet men. Now, my sister. She always meets men like you."

Drew took her hand and tucked it in the crook of his elbow. She had such delicate fingers, he wanted to stop and examine them more closely, to memorize every little detail that made her so perfect. "Men like me? And what kind of man am I?"

She gave him a sideways glance. "You're not married, are you?"

Drew shook his head, suddenly captivated by her eyes. He wanted to pull her to a stop and stare into those green depths until he could see right into her soul. Who was this woman? And where had she been hiding all these years?

"You don't have any psychological problems, haven't spend any time in state institutions? You don't dress in ladies' underwear? You're not sexually attracted to my shoes? You don't play the ponies or watch ESPN twenty-four hours a day?"

He shook his head again. The truth be told, he wouldn't have admitted any vice that might have hurt his chances with her. He'd be a choirboy if it meant the opportunity to spend more time with Tess Ryan.

"Then you're the kind of man I never meet," Tess said with a wry grin.

"Maybe your luck has changed," he replied, giving her fingers a gentle squeeze.

They set off down the sidewalk, chatting amiably, laughing and teasing, a feeling of instant familiarity settling between them. Considering how he'd almost skipped this evening's party, the night had taken a decided turn for the better. They'd walked nearly two blocks, when Drew stopped short just a few feet from his car.

He cursed softly as he stared at the front passenger side of the black BMW sedan. "Damn. Look at that! I've got a flat tire." He bent down and shook his head slowly. "These are brand-new tires."

"The back tire is flat, too," Tess said.

With another curse, he straightened, then circled the car. "They're all flat! Someone slashed them."

With a worried frown, Tess looked down the street, then back at Drew's car. "Your car is the only one. Why would someone slash your tires and no one else's?"

Drew reached into his jacket pocket and pulled out his cell phone. Everything was going so well and now this glitch. He'd be damned if he was going to let four flat tires put an end to his evening with Tess. "I'll call the auto club and they'll come out right away. This will just take a minute. Then we can go in your car."

He hit the memory dial and waited for the service rep to ask his name. "This is Andrew Wyatt," he said, sending Tess an apologetic smile as he dug for his membership card in his wallet.

But she didn't return his smile. Instead, her eyes went wide and she gasped softly. "Andrew? I—I thought your name was Drew."

He held his hand over the phone, the look of concern on her face causing a brief flicker of alarm. "Drew. Short for Andrew," he explained. He'd assumed she knew his name. After all, it was listed in the evening's program, and Marceline Lavery must have mentioned it to her. There were even photos of him and the other board members in the hallway leading to the reception area. No wonder she was acting so strangely, Drew mused. He'd never formally introduced himself.

The operator came back on the line and he turned his attention back to the car. "I'm parked two blocks west of the art museum on Clairmont. I've got four flat tires and I need you to send a truck right away."

"Are—are you an architect?" Tess asked.

He nodded, listening to the instructions from the auto club and watching the strange play of emotions across her face. What had caused her sudden change in mood? The warmth that had grown between them had been replaced by a chill breeze.

"I—I have to go," Tess said, slowly backing away. "I'm sorry, I just remembered, I do have other plans."

Drew frowned, stepping toward her. "Wait. We'll leave the car and call a cab. It will only take a few minutes."

"No," Tess said, shaking her head. "I really need to go. But thanks for the invitation. It—it was nice meeting you, Mr.—er, Drew."

With a soft oath, he told the service rep to wait, then pulled the phone away from his ear. But she was already halfway down the block and retreating at a quick pace. "Tess! Come on. What's wrong?"

"Nothing," she called. "I just have to go. Have a nice evening!"

"I'll walk you to your car!"

"No, no. I'm fine."

Drew leaned back against the BMW and watched Tess disappear into the night. Rubbing his forehead, he tried to figure out what had just transpired. One moment, he and Tess were getting along great. The next, she was in full retreat with some excuse about "other plans." What had he done? What had he said to send her off at a run?

"First the fish, then the dog. And now, a beautiful woman," Drew muttered. "What the hell is wrong with me?"

"WHAT ARE THE CHANCES?" Tess grumbled as she pulled her house keys from her purse. "Andrew is a common name. And there are hundreds of architects in the city of Atlanta." But how many architects named Andrew Wyatt ran in the rarefied social circle that Lucy found so appealing?

"He called himself Drew," she said, pushing the key into the lock. "And Lucy called him Andy." Besides, she distinctly remembered Lucy saying that her Andy had brown eyes. And Tess's Drew had blue eyes. Then there was the comment about the dimple in his chin. Drew Wyatt didn't have a dimple in his chin, nor was he "cute," a description that Lucy had used more than once. Puppies were cute. Drew Wyatt was devastatingly, breathtakingly handsome.

"It's just a coincidence," Tess murmured. But that explanation lasted just as long as it took for her to open the front door. Lucy was standing on the other side, her eyes bright, her smile broad. She wore a pink cashmere sweater set littered with dead leaves, her favorite string of pearls and immaculately pressed khakis with muddy knees.

"I did it!" she said, grabbing Tess's elbow and pulling her into the living room.

"Did what?"

"Closure," Lucy said. "I called Andy's office and his secretary told me that he was at the art museum for some la-di-da reception. So I went over and found his car. And I let all the air out of his tires. He is so pathological about that stupid car. It serves him right."

Tess's heart sank as all her fears were confirmed. What *were* the odds? The first interesting man she meets in almost two years and he's the scum-sucking scoundrel that dumped her little sister!

"I feel empowered. I feel liberated," Lucy cried, twirling around the coffee table. "And I feel naughty, too."

Tess rubbed the knot of tension that gripped her forehead, trying to resolve the mass of contradictions swirling in her mind. Drew Wyatt couldn't be that bad, could he? He seemed like such a nice guy to have done all the reprehensible things that Lucy claimed. Could Lucy have misunderstood his actions, misread his motives? "Luce, I don't think you should—"

"Oh, pooh," Lucy said. "Don't be such a spoilsport. Besides, he'll just call the auto club and they'll come and fix his tires. I wish I could have seen his face."

Tess *had* seen his face and he'd been more than just a little put off. In fact, he'd been downright angry, though she wanted to believe it wasn't as much for the tires as their spoiled date. "This could be considered vandalism," Tess said.

"No," Lucy replied. "Dumping paint on his car would probably be vandalism." A wicked smile curled her lips and she trembled with suppressed excitement.

Tess regarded her warily. "What? Did you throw paint on his car?"

Lucy glanced at her watch. "Not quite yet. But it should be happening very soon."

"What did you do, Luce?"

Lucy grabbed Tess's hand and led her over to the sofa, then tugged her down beside her. "After I let the air out of his tires, I went to his house and rigged up another surprise." She lowered her voice. "I put a couple of gallons of old paint up on the brick pillars beside his front gate. And then I tied the handles of the cans to the gate with some rope. And when the gate swings open, *voilà!* The cans will fly off the pillars and dump on his car!" Lucy threw her arms around Tess's neck. "This was such a good idea, Tess! What can we do to him next? Something really nasty and hateful.''

Tess shoved away from her sister. "We'll do nothing! This is where it stops, Luce. You've damaged property and that's against the law."

"He can wash the paint off," Lucy said with a shrug.

"You used latex paint?"

Her sister frowned. "What's latex? I used some of the old paint that was out in the garden shed. The stuff that the gardener uses to paint the patio furniture. That washes off, doesn't it?"

"No, it doesn't. Do you realize what could happen? The police could get your fingerprints off the cans and they could arrest you and throw you in jail." Tess raked her fingers through her hair, then cursed silently. This was all her fault. She should never have egged Lucy on. Lucy was always excessive, and her vendetta against Andrew Wyatt was no exception.

Lucy waved her hand dismissively. "I don't care. It's worth a few nights in the slammer. Now, I think this calls for champagne," she said. "I found a wonderful bottle of Cristal in Daddy's wine cellar. We'll have a little celebration. And then we can plan our next step."

Tess pulled her keys out of her purse and stood up. "Actually, Luce, I just remembered I forgot something at the office. I—I'll be back in a little while." She headed for the door, then stopped short and looked back at her sister. "Don't do anything else until I get back, all right?"

As the front door closed behind her, Tess's mind began to race. First she'd need to find Andrew Wyatt's home address. Then she'd need to get to his house before he did. And then she'd have to undo Lucy's damage before it actually became a criminal offense.

She ran to her car and pulled her briefcase out of the

trunk. Inside was a list of all the guests at the party. Thankfully, she found Andrew Wyatt's name on the last page and beside it an address in Dunwoody, a lovely residential suburb. If her luck held, she could get to his house before he did and defuse Lucy's paint-can bomb.

The traffic was light at that time of night and Tess managed the ten-mile drive to Andrew Wyatt's house in less than twenty minutes. "Let's hope the auto club responds to a guy with a BMW as slowly as they do to a woman with a ten-year-old Toyota," she muttered, squinting in the darkness for the correct house number. As she slowed in front of his gates, she noticed the paint cans perched on either pillar and breathed a sigh of relief.

Tess parked her car on the far side of the street and hopped out. The neighborhood was dark and quiet and she heard a dog bark in the distance. Lucy had mentioned a dog. All she needed now was a slavering Doberman nipping at her fingers through the gate. "Just keep calm," she murmured. "You have plenty of time."

The paint cans were well out of reach and Tess stared up at the pillars, wondering how her sister had managed to get them up there without a ladder. With a soft oath, she pulled the tight skirt of her cocktail dress up around her thighs, kicked off her shoes and grabbed hold of the iron fence. Slowly she shimmied up the fence until she was level with the top of the pillar.

The rope was tied tightly to the handle of the can and she worked at it for nearly a minute. "I should have untied the rope from the gate," she muttered in hindsight. "Think, Tess! Think!"

When she finally had the can in hand, she slowly slid back down, avoiding the bush in front of the pillar and careful not to spill a drop of paint on the tidy brick driveway. Tess glanced at her watch as she moved to the second pillar. She had almost begun to climb again, when she remembered to untie the rope at the gate.

"Come on, Tess. Don't screw up now. You created this monster, you're going to have to deal with her now." Why had she ever mentioned the concept of closure to Lucy? Why hadn't she just let her sister spend the night under her bed, weeping and wailing as she usually did? Why couldn't she just mind her own business and leave Lucy to deal with her own problems?

"Why, why, why?" Tess muttered. "Because you're a softhearted fool. And you've made it your life's mission to look after Lucy's happiness." She shimmied up to the top of the second pillar and reached out to grab the paint can. Her fingers were just closing around the handle when she heard a soft growl. She looked down to see a dog on the other side of the fence, eyeing her toes with drooling delight.

With a soft scream, Tess pulled her foot up. But the quick movement threw her off balance and she felt herself falling backward. She grabbed at anything she could as she fell, coming up with the rope attached to the paint can. As if in slow motion, she tumbled into the bushes, her stunned gaze fixed on the paint can that was rapidly descending after her.

Tess landed with a thud in the greenery. And the paint can landed on her stomach, splattering white paint over her face and shoulders and legs and knocking the wind out of her. She pushed up, gasping, wiping the white goo from her face and wincing at the feel of it dripping off her hair. Just then, headlights struck the bush and she ducked down.

The black BMW slowly pulled to a stop, tires now fully inflated. Drew reached for the remote on the visor, then waited as the gates opened. Tess held her breath, praying that she hadn't been seen. The car rolled forward and she lay back into the foliage and groaned, the clank of the closing gate a fitting punctuation to her little adventure. How he had missed her she couldn't begin to imagine. After all, she looked like Casper the Friendly Ghost, all white and luminous in the dark of night.

Tess felt something wet on her hand and she turned to find the dog, his nose through the fence, happily licking at her elbow—the only paint-free spot on her body. With a cry, she snatched her arm away. "Shoo," she hissed. "Go away! Scoot!" The dog cocked its head, woofed, then turned and trotted toward the house in a clumsy gait.

She wasn't sure how long she stayed in the bushes. Her watch face was covered with white paint. But when she was certain she was safe from Andrew Wyatt and his vicious, elbow-licking dog, she scrambled to her feet, grabbed her shoes and skulked across the street to her car.

Before she got inside, she forced herself to remove her ruined dress and panty hose. She might be covered with wet paint, but she wasn't about to get it all over the inside of her car. Though she wasn't sure how she'd explain her lack of clothing and her pale complexion if she got stopped by the police, she was sure she'd come up with something less ridiculous than the truth.

She slid behind the wheel and turned on the ignition, catching sight of herself in the rearview mirror. "This is the last time I save your skinny little butt, Lucy Ryan," she muttered. "The very last time!"

"I DON'T SEE why you had to mess everything up!"

Tess placed her hands on her desk and met Lucy's petulant expression with thinly veiled anger. "Look at me!" she said. "I still haven't gotten all the paint off my face!"

"You look fashionably pale," Lucy countered. "And pale is very chic this year."

"I don't care what's in fashion! I was trying to save your butt, Lucy. And all the thanks I get for my trouble is your incessant whining. If your little act of revenge would have worked, you could have ended up in jail!"

Lucy slouched back into her chair and pouted. "Why are you in such a bad mood?"

"I have a splitting headache. Maybe it's all the fumes from the mineral spirits. I practically had to take a bath in it and I still don't have all the paint out of my hair." Lucy opened her mouth and Tess stopped her words with a warning hand. "Don't you dare tell me that streaked hair is in this year."

"Well, I don't care if you *are* mad. I feel wonderful. I'd feel even more wonderful if Andy Wyatt's car were covered with white paint, instead of my sister. But I still feel like I've made a positive step toward my imminent happiness. I'm not quite there yet, but—"

"This is it," Tess warned, standing up to pace the confines of her office. "This is all the closure you need. You're over him and you're going to get on with your life."

Lucy smoothed the skirt of her designer suit, then opened her purse. "I'll let you know about that," she said, plucking her compact out.

Tess narrowed her eyes and was about to launch into another round of threats and warnings when her intercom buzzed. She snatched up the phone and punched the button, waiting for her assistant to respond.

"Tess, there's a man out here to see you. He says he knows you."

She reached across the desk and flipped her calendar to the correct day. "I don't have any appointments this morning. And I don't have time to see any sales reps. Get his card and tell him to call for an appointment."

She heard Clarise clear her throat and waited for her response. "What should I tell him to do with his tray of crab claws?"

Tess swallowed convulsively. "Crab claws?"

Lucy looked up from powdering her nose. "I adore crab claws."

"I'll just send him away," Clarise said.

Tess sucked in a sharp breath and held it, her gaze darting to Lucy who was about to head for the door. "Wait!" she cried.

Lucy turned and gave her an inquisitive look. "I have to go. I have a hair appointment."

Tess crossed the office, the phone still to her ear, and grabbed Lucy's arm. "Clarise, I want you to take our guest into the coffee room and have him put his tray into the refrigerator. And then I want you to offer him a cup of coffee. And do it very, very slowly."

Tess dropped the phone back in the cradle and forced a smile. "Wait just a second," she said as she hurried to her office door. "I'll walk you out."

She opened the door a crack and watched as Drew Wyatt strolled past her office and down the hall to the coffee room. When he was safely inside, she grabbed Lucy's hand and hauled her across the reception area and out the front door, her heart racing as fast as her mind.

The very last thing she needed right now was a huge emotional confrontation between Lucy and Drew. Knowing the state Lucy was in, there would probably be shouting and recriminations and threats. And after that was over, Tess would be forced to explain what Lucy's former boyfriend was doing in *her* office, bearing a gift of expensive seafood.

"What is your problem?" Lucy cried, yanking away from Tess.

"I don't have a problem! But you will if you do anything else to Andrew Wyatt. Do you understand?"

"But I—"

"Lucy, I'll call the police myself. And that's a promise. Now, go visit your hairdresser and think about what I said."

Her sister stuck out her lower lip and narrowed her eyes. "Are you trying to get rid of me?"

"Luce, I've got a business to run and clients to call. I'll talk to you when I get home."

Tess held her breath until Lucy walked out the front door, then turned back to her office. This was more than she could handle. Lucy dropping in to visit, Drew stopping by with food. It was time to put an end to the mess she had made!

Gathering her resolve, she stalked into the office and headed toward the kitchen. She found Drew there, watching bemusedly as Clarise poured the world's most meticulously prepared cup of coffee. "Mr. Wyatt!"

He spun around and his gaze skimmed over her features in a familiar, almost casual way. She felt as if she'd been touched, a slow warmth seeping through her veins. A lazy smile curled his lips. "Tess!"

Clarise looked visibly relieved. She quickly finished making his coffee, pushed the mug in Drew's direction and hurried out of the room. Drew's gaze followed her and he grinned when he came back to Tess. "Good morning," he said, his voice warm and soothing to her ragged nerves.

"Good morning," Tess replied. Her mind suddenly went blank and she tried to think of something witty to say. "Wha—what are you doing here?"

"I thought I'd stop by and see you." He frowned slightly and stepped forward. "Are you all right? You look a little pale."

Tess shook her head, tucking a strand of hair behind her ear as she groaned inwardly. Considering the fact that she'd been doused with white paint, she could count on being "a little pale" for a few weeks longer. "I'm just tired. I didn't sleep much last night."

"Neither did I," he murmured. He took another step closer, close enough for her to catch a whiff of his cologne. She wanted to close her eyes and revel in the scent. "I was thinking about you all night."

"Oh," Tess breathed. "No, that's not why I couldn't sleep. I—I mean, I was thinking about you, but that's...not..." She took a long, steadying breath. Stick to polite chitchat, she told herself. "So, what brings you here?"

"I was hoping you'd have lunch with me. After that fiasco last night, I—"

"Fiasco?"

"The flat tires. Remember, we were going to have coffee. I thought we might start again with lunch."

Tess glanced over at the tray of crab claws, then back at Drew. "I'm really not very hungry. But maybe another time?"

Drew stared into her eyes for a long moment, a scowl creasing his forehead. "Is everything all right? You ran off so quickly last night. We didn't get a chance to talk."

Tess turned and idly began to rearrange the coffee mugs on the counter. "No, actually, everything isn't all right. I—I appreciate the invitation to lunch, but I really don't think we should see each other socially."

She felt his hand on her arm and he slowly turned her toward him. "Why? I thought we were—"

"Well, we weren't," Tess said, avoiding his eyes. "At least, I wasn't. You're just not my type." *You're Lucy's type*, she added silently. The type that would unceremoniously dump a poor, besotted girl with no explanation. The type that would profess his love, then break a girl's heart into a million pieces. "You're...I don't know. I just know that dating you would be a mistake."

Drew raked his fingers through his hair and shook his head. "I don't get it, Tess. We're obviously attracted to each other. I couldn't have been mistaken about that. You're not married, I'm not married. What's the problem?"

"How do you know I'm not involved?" she asked, tipping her chin up defensively. "I could be dating someone. Seriously."

His jaw tightened. "Are you?"

"That's not the point."

"Then what is?" he asked, a trace of frustration creeping into his voice.

"The point..." Tess cleared her throat. "The point is that I'm very busy. I have some important calls to make and I don't have time to explain. But I'm not interested in...getting involved...with you...with anyone." Tess walked toward the door. "So, why don't I show you out and we can just forget we ever met?"

Tess turned, but he stopped her, grabbing her shoulders and giving them a gentle squeeze. A warm tingle wound through her limbs, making her knees soft and her arms weak. How could she resist him? There was no denying the attraction racing through her. Overwhelming attraction. Attraction that made her knees wobble and her hands shake. In truth, she'd never been more attracted to a man in her life.

Tess groaned inwardly. This was wrong! Had he been

anyone but Lucy's ex-boyfriend, she might have thrown her arms around his neck and kissed him. But he was Andy Wyatt. And she was Lucy Ryan's careful and conservative sister. To have even a single romantic thought in his direction was a betrayal of her sister's trust. Never mind that he made her blood run hot and her pulse pound. That was completely beside the point.

"I'm not going to give up," he said, turning her around and bending nearer.

Tess knew if she looked up into his eyes he'd kiss her. His mouth was so close she could feel his warm breath on her cheek. "And I'm not going to change my mind," she countered, her gaze fixed on the paisley pattern of his tie.

Drew sighed, then let his hands slide down her arms and drop to his sides. He stepped around her and looked into her eyes. "Maybe it's time to gamble a little bit, Tess. After all, what do you have to lose?"

With that, he walked away, striding through her office and out the front door. Tess watched him from the doorway of the coffee room, her arms wrapped around her. "What do I have to lose?" she murmured. "Only my heart." She drew in a long breath and banished his image from her mind. "Only my heart...and my sister."

3

"I'M A NICE GUY, aren't I? Why wouldn't she want to go out with me?"

Drew leaned back in his chair and kicked his feet up on the edge of his drawing board. His business manager, Elliot Cosgrove, sat across from him, his briefcase open on his lap, sheaves of papers clutched in his hands.

Cosgrove had worked for Wyatt and Associates for nearly ten years. He'd become a trusted employee, a man Drew counted on to run the firm while he was out of town on project work. Elliot had a talent for keeping track of money and deadlines, and Drew had come to depend on his good judgment in all matters. But until now, he'd never asked Elliot's advice on women.

Cosgrove was a long shot. Drew would probably be better off asking a monk for dating advice. And it wasn't as if he and Elliot were close friends. Drew called Elliot by his first name, Elliot called Drew "sir." But after last night, Drew was willing to listen to any opinion he could solicit.

"I'm going to need you to sign the Gresham Park contracts today so I can messenger them over to the developer's attorney, sir," Elliot said, fumbling with his papers. "And we have the preliminary meeting with the civic center committee in ten minutes. I've had Kim put copies of the proposal and your sketches in the conference room. The committee members should be here any minute."

Drew steepled his fingers and scowled. "Most women think I'm a real catch," he continued. "I don't mean to brag, but sometimes I have more women than I can handle."

Elliot looked up, pushing his wire-rimmed glasses up the bridge of his nose, his brown eyes wide. "I wouldn't know about that, sir. I've never had that particular problem. In my experience, one woman is usually one more than I can handle."

"Maybe I was moving too fast," Drew speculated. "I was pushing too hard. It's just that I've never met anyone like Tess before. She's beautiful and smart and sexy. She says what she thinks. She doesn't play games."

"Games, sir? Like tennis and squash?" Elliot scratched his head, then went back to studying his papers, clenching his pencil in his teeth. "I've heard that Lubich is putting together a bid for the civic center project as well," he mumbled offhandedly.

"You know how women are," Drew said. "They twist you around until you don't know which side is up. And you try to figure them out, but that's like trying to build a house with nothing but feathers. The wind changes and what have you got?"

Elliot looked perplexed, pulling the pencil from his teeth. "I don't know. A lot of feathers?"

"Nothing," Drew replied, straightening in his chair and slapping his hands on the desk. "You've got nothing. Do you have a woman in your life, Cosgrove?"

"I—I do," he stammered. "I did. I mean, I have had...just one. But it didn't work out. We had to break up. It was inevitable." He blushed, then glanced down into his briefcase. "Lubich could cause problems, sir."

"And why is that?" Drew asked distractedly.

"You know the man stops at nothing to squash the competition, and last time we were—"

"No, why did you break up?"

"I—I wasn't the man she thought I was," Elliot mumbled. "Now, about these contracts. I think we should—"

"But Tess doesn't know who I am. We've barely spent an hour in each other's company and already she's decided she doesn't want anything to do with me. That's what I can't figure out. I usually make a good first impression. Some women call me charming." He paused and stared at his reflection in the window behind his drawing board. "Maybe I had something in my teeth."

"You are very charming, sir, and your teeth are perfect," Elliot commented with a bit too much enthusiasm. He realized what he'd said and forced a wan smile. "Maybe we should talk about your trip to Tokyo."

Drew was loath to switch subjects. He still hadn't a clue what to do about Tess Ryan. In all honesty, he'd never met a woman who *wasn't* attracted to him. This odd turn of events completely baffled him.

But it wasn't only that she had rejected him. He could certainly handle rejection. What worried him most was that he couldn't stop thinking about her. From the moment they met, he'd decided that Tess Ryan was someone special. He'd replayed the short conversations they'd shared, he'd imagined her voice and pictured her face too many times to count. He needed to look into her pretty green eyes again, to touch her and tease her and make her laugh.

He could send flowers, truckloads of flowers. But Drew sensed that wouldn't work. Jewelry appealed to some women and he was certain Tess would look stunning in diamonds, but diamonds were a bit ahead of the game. He was at a complete loss. All he knew was that it would take something very special to get Tess to change her opinion of him. And to make any headway at all, he'd need to see her again.

Drew grabbed his phone and buzzed his assistant. He bounced a pencil on the drawing board as he waited for her to answer. "Kim, I need you to get me some information. I want you to go through those invitations I left on your desk. Then I want you to call and find out if Tess Ryan at Parties Perfect is coordinating any of those events this weekend. And if you find a party that she's planning, I want you to R.S.V.P. for me. Let them know that I'd be happy to attend."

Drew smiled smugly as he hung up the phone. Tess didn't want to see him socially. But that didn't mean he couldn't run into her while she was working. A simple solution to a complex problem. "She'll have to see me now," he said. "She won't have a choice."

"You're going out with Tess *Ryan?*" Elliot asked. "The party lady?"

Drew leaned back in his chair again and sighed. "I have aspirations to go out with her, Elliot. Right now, our relationship is a little one-sided. Do you know her?"

Elliot shook his head. "I—I think I might know her sister."

"I didn't know she had a sister."

"Maybe she doesn't," Elliot replied, his expression anxious and his voice edgy. "Maybe I'm thinking of someone else. Can we talk about Tokyo now?"

Drew shrugged. "All right. How did everything go here while I was gone?"

Elliot cleared his throat. "My—my car broke down, so I used your BMW for a few days. I—I hope that was all right."

"No problem. It's leased to the business anyway."

"And I put in an appearance at the symphony fund-raiser last month," he added. "I thought since—"

"Good," Drew said. "Better someone uses the tickets the firm bought."

"And—and I stayed in your guest room while my apartment was being painted. In fact, I've been staying there for the past month."

Drew frowned. "You've been living at my house?"

Elliot grew red around the collar. "I—I'm sorry. But it—it was Rufus, sir. I didn't have a choice. He was so distraught."

Drew blinked. "Rufus? My dog?"

"Yes, sir. I don't mean to intrude in your family life, but I believe Rufus is having problems. And I think it stems from all that television he watches with your house-keeper. While I was staying with him, I got him started on an exercise program. We spent a lot of time outdoors. And we talked about his feelings."

"You talked to my dog? Please don't tell me he talked back. Because if you tell me that, Elliot, I'm going to have to find myself another business manager."

A soft knock sounded on Drew's office door and Kim interrupted their conversation with an apologetic smile. "Mr. Wyatt, there's a policewoman here to see you. And Mr. Eugene and his committee are here from the civic center board."

Drew sighed. "I'll be right out."

Elliot frowned in concern. "A policewoman, sir?"

"Someone vandalized my car last night," Drew explained, waving off his worry. "Let all the air out of my tires. I called the police, but I didn't think they'd follow up so soon."

Elliot followed Drew and Kim into the reception area of the office suite. The members of the civic center committee were comfortably settled in the guest chairs and the policewoman waited next to Kim's desk. When she saw Drew, she smiled and approached him.

"Mr. Andrew Wyatt?"

"Yes. Did you find the kids who tampered with my car? I want to press charges if you did."

She stepped toward him until she was only inches away. Then her gaze dropped, slowly, to his crotch. "Is that a weapon in your pocket, big boy, or are you just happy to see me?"

With that, she tossed down the duffel bag she was carrying, reached inside, and a moment later, a raucous bump and grind filled the room. When she turned back to Drew, she grabbed the collar of her blue shirt and ripped it open to reveal a sexy black bra and an unnaturally generous display of cleavage.

The world seemed to grind to a halt as the reality of the situation sank in. This was no policewoman! Elliot gasped and clutched his briefcase in front of him, as if it offered some protection. The civic center committee went wide-eyed and slack-jawed. Kim buried her face in her hands, clearly unwilling to watch the show unfolding before them. And Drew was...utterly speechless.

By the time the stripper had peeled down to her skimpy panties, he couldn't help chuckling at the sheer absurdity of the situation. Every move the dancer made was meant to tease and tantalize, but it had exactly the opposite effect on everyone who watched. Faces flushed, the committee members squirmed in their chairs, not sure whether they should enjoy the show or muster up a little moral outrage.

Drew had only one question—besides the question of whether they were real or not. What he wanted to know was how a half-naked exotic dancer had ended up in his office lobby. It wasn't his birthday and he could think of no other occasion that would warrant such an appearance, no buddies who might pull such a trashy stunt. He winced as she bent over and waved to the committee from between her legs, wiggling her backside provocatively.

"Lubich," he murmured, remembering Elliot's warning. The man would stop at nothing to destroy the competition. The last time they squared off as competitors on a shopping mall project, Lubich had started a rumor that Wyatt and Associates specified substandard materials in their last job. Lubich was slimy and underhanded, but Drew wouldn't have thought him the type to pull a silly trick like this.

But then, the spotless reputation of Wyatt and Associates was hard to sully without solid proof. Maybe Lubich was desperate, Drew mused as he reached into his jacket pocket and withdrew his wallet. When the stripper turned her attention back to him, he pressed a fifty-dollar bill into her hand. "I think that'll just about do it."

She smiled, wrapped her arms around his neck and kissed him full on the mouth. "I'm glad you enjoyed me," she said. "I'm available for private performances, too."

He held out another fifty. "Who sent you?"

A smile curled her lushly painted lips and she shook her head. "That's a little secret."

Drew untangled himself from her arms then helped her retrieve the clothes she had scattered over the reception area. Gently, he guided her to the door and opened it for her. He felt compelled to question her further, to offer her a bigger bribe, but he also wanted to get her out of the office as fast as she could shimmy. "You have a nice day now," he said, giving her a friendly smile.

When he turned back to the clients who waited in the reception area, Drew wasn't sure what to say. Should he pretend that nothing had happened? From the looks on their faces, that might be a stretch. Or should he try to explain? Hell, a beautiful woman just ripped her clothes off in the middle of his office. Beyond that, he wasn't sure of all the particulars.

"Mom is always popping in at the oddest times," Drew finally muttered in a dry apology. "Usually she brings cookies."

The committee members glanced nervously at each other, unsure of how to take his comment. Then a slow chuckle began with Mr. Eugene and rippled through the group. A few seconds later, all five men were laughing heartily and recounting their favorite parts of the dance. Relieved, Drew directed them toward the conference room, then turned back to Kim and Elliot.

"I want to know who sent the stripper. If you can't find out, hire a private detective to find out."

"You mean, you don't know?" Elliot asked.

"Of course not! Though I suspect it might be a couple of Lubich's lackeys. They might be the ones who let the air out of my tires, too. I'm beginning to think that wasn't a random act."

"Would you like me to work on the Tess Ryan project or the stripper project?" Kim asked in her usual efficient manner.

Drew cursed softly and shook his head. His assistant should be working on the civic center bid, but Drew had more pressing problems. "You work on Tess," he said, nodding at Kim. "Elliot, you work on the stripper. I'll expect some answers from both of you by the end of business today."

With that, Drew turned and strode toward the conference room. He'd spent entirely too much time today think-

ing about women, both clothed and unclothed. It was time
to get back to work.

"HAPPY BIRTHDAY to you!"

A wave of applause broke out and Tess smiled as she
stood behind the birthday cake shaped like the head of a
longhorn cow. Party guests, dressed in western attire,
watched as the birthday boy took a deep breath and blew
out the fifty candles she had so painstakingly lit moments
before. Another round of cheers went up and Arthur Duvelle's wife, Eleanor, kissed him on the cheek.

The party had turned out to be one of Tess's best. She'd
set up hay wagons for the buffet dinner, and bales of straw
provided casual seating throughout the large backyard.
The caterers served up tasty barbecue and a country-
western band provided foot-stomping music. She'd even
hired two rodeo cowboys to perform rope tricks, and a
few adventurous guests tried their luck on a mechanical
bull.

"Great party."

Tess turned to accept the compliment from the gentleman behind her. But as she caught sight of his face, her
breath froze in her throat. "Wha—what are you doing
here?"

Drew stepped up beside her and gazed out at the guests,
a smug grin on his face. "I missed you," he said. "I had
to see you."

"This is a private party! You can't just walk in here
and expect to get away with it!" Tess glanced over at the
host and hostess of the party, then back at Drew. "You
have to go! Now!"

"But I don't want to go."

Tess watched nervously as Arthur Duvelle turned and
motioned to her. It was time to cut the cake, a responsi-

bility that she would cover. But before she could get down to business, she had to get rid of Drew. "Please," she said. "Just tell me what you want, then go."

He crossed his arms over his chest and pondered the question for an excruciatingly long moment. The fabric of his chambray work shirt stretched across his broad shoulders. Tess's eyes drifted down to his narrow waist, to the faded jeans that hugged his long legs. If it was possible, he looked better in work clothes than he did in a tuxedo.

She ignored the flutter of desire in her stomach, writing it off to an overindulgence in barbecue. She couldn't afford to dwell on the fantasies that flashed in her mind, like how long it would take to rip that shirt open with her teeth...or whether she could unfasten his jeans with just one hand...and whether the light dusting of hair at his collar led all the way down to his— She swallowed hard. The butterflies in her stomach had turned into a beached flounder, slamming up against her rib cage until she felt nauseated.

"Well, what do you want?" she prodded, trying to keep the flounder from affecting her voice.

"I want you to go out with me," he said in a tone so matter-of-fact that he might have been commenting on the weather. "Dinner. Maybe a movie?"

Tess knew she should refuse, but right now she was desperate to get him out of her party. "All right," she said. "I promise. If you'll leave, I'll go out with you."

A slow smile curled his lips, sending a shiver down her spine. "When?" he asked, his dark eyebrow arching.

"Whenever. Call my office tomorrow morning and we'll pick a night. Now go!"

Just then, Arthur Duvelle moved away from the cake and started in Tess's direction. "Go," she pleaded.

But Duvelle had already caught sight of Drew and approached them with a scowl. Tess's heart froze and her mind scrambled for a plausible excuse. She would tell him that Drew was helping her with decorations...or the catering...or the music. With a soft cry, she grabbed a tray from the table beside her and shoved it into Drew's hands.

"Wyatt? Is that you?" Duvelle pushed his cowboy hat back on his head, then broke into a wide grin. "Well, hell, it is!"

Drew stepped forward and held out his hand, balancing the tray on his other palm. "Arthur! Happy birthday! I know you've probably heard this already, but you don't look a day over thirty."

Duvelle pumped Drew's hand. "You rascal! And you still know how to get on my good side. Eleanor told me you wouldn't be coming. She said you were in Tokyo."

"I got back a few days ago," Drew said. "I couldn't miss another chance to look at one of my favorite projects." He turned toward the house. "When are you going to let me add that conservatory for Eleanor?"

"We'll talk," Arthur said, clapping Drew on the shoulder. "Eleanor's birthday is coming up. Might make a nice gift, don't you think?"

Drew chuckled. "I'll sharpen my pencil and start making some sketches."

With that, Arthur stepped into the crowd and began to mingle, leaving Tess to contemplate the cake knife she clutched in her hand—and how it might look imbedded in Drew Wyatt's blackmailing heart. Why did he always find a way to prick her sense of propriety? And why did she always assume the worst of him? She grabbed the tray he held and slammed it back down on the table.

"Should I fear for my life?" Drew murmured, leaning close and lowering his voice. "Or will you forgive me my little deception?"

Tess sighed in exasperation, then moved to the table. With precise movements, she began to slice the cake and plop each piece onto a plate. "You tricked me," she said, handing a portion to a guest.

Drew chuckled as he reached out and swiped a bit of butter-cream frosting. "And you made another incorrect assumption. I was invited to this party. I didn't crash."

"You hate parties. What made you decide to come to this one?"

He popped the frosting into his mouth. "I like coming to *your* parties."

"And how do you know Arthur Duvelle?"

"I designed his house. I've also designed three of his office complexes. We're old friends." Drew grabbed her elbow. "Such old friends that I'm sure he wouldn't mind if I stole you away from your duties for a few minutes."

Tess dropped the knife, satisfied that she'd provided enough dessert for the guests. She wiped her hands on a towel and turned to Drew. "All right," she said with a tight smile. "I can spare a few minutes."

Drew grabbed her hand and laced her fingers through his. They strolled along the edges of the gardens and Tess fixed her attention on the azaleas. "So, I guess we have a date," she said. "Even though it was secured through trickery and blackmail, I still agreed to a date. Unless you're feeling remorseful and will release me from my promise."

Drew pulled her to a stop and turned her to face him. "Why are you so determined to avoid me?"

His words betrayed his frustration. Tess's feelings matched his own. Why was he so determined to see her? "There are probably hundreds, maybe even thousands of women in the greater Atlanta area who would love to go out with you," she said.

"Why aren't you one of them?" Drew asked.

"I told you, you're not my type. It's as simple as that. I know your ego won't let you believe that, but try."

"You don't know me. I'm a nice guy. Ask Arthur and Eleanor. They'll vouch for me."

Tess laughed. "I doubt that. And you may think you're a nice guy, but you've probably broken hundreds of hearts. Guys like you can't avoid it."

"I haven't had a date in six months," Drew said defensively. "Any hearts that might have been broken are well mended by now."

Tess's jaw tightened. Good grief, he'd say anything to get into her good graces. Oh, if there were only a way to pay him back for all the pain he'd caused Lucy. If only she could get him to fall in love with her as hard and as fast as Lucy had fallen for him. Then she'd dump him like a bad habit! After that, they could discuss broken hearts.

"So you're a little desperate?" she asked, silently considering such a plan.

Drew sighed and grabbed her shoulders. "Tess, from the first time I saw you, I was desperate. Desperate to get to know you. You're smart and beautiful and I—"

"Flattery will get you nowhere," Tess said. But in truth, it was getting him everywhere. If she didn't know Andrew Wyatt for the rogue he was, she might actually believe him. Part of her wanted to believe that he was attracted to her for all the right reasons. But how could she attribute anything to him but the worst characteristics the male sex had to offer?

"It's not flattery," he said. "I'm not going to lie to you just to get you to go out with me."

Oh, what a scoundrel! What a creep! "All right," Tess

said slyly. "One date. And if I decide there won't be a second, you have to respect my wishes. Deal?"

"Somehow, I get the idea that you'd agree to a root canal with much more enthusiasm."

"Oh, I'm looking forward to our date," she countered. Though not for the same reason he was. She had already begun to formulate a plan, perfect retribution for making Lucy so miserable. But she'd need to be very careful. There was a fine line to tread, leading him on yet keeping him at a safe distance. She'd have to make him believe that she was as interested as he was, and when the time was right, she'd toss him aside.

It would probably be easier to simply seduce him. To drag him into bed, drive him mad with passion, then boot him out of her life. But Tess didn't have that much faith in her abilities in the bedroom. Given her rather limited experience in the seductive arts, she couldn't guarantee that he'd want more than a one-night stand. And unless she left him wanting more, the plan wouldn't work.

No, making him fall in love with her would be a much better option. Of course, it could take longer. But she'd already made some progress. He'd insisted on a first date. And her hard-to-get attitude seemed to pique his interest even more. Tess forced a smile. "You'll call me?"

He nodded. And then, without warning, he bent down and brushed his lips against her cheek. "I think I better leave while I'm ahead. I'll call you."

He drew his palm over the spot were his kiss had been just moments before, and smiled. He left her standing near the birdbath, her fingertips tracing the faint warm outline of his lips. A delicious heat seeped through her body.

She shouldn't have liked the way his lips felt...but she did. She shouldn't have craved a more intimate kiss, but she couldn't help it. And she never should have agreed to dinner, for dinner might lead to something more, something she might not be able to resist.

Determination. That's all it would take to control her feelings. And she'd simply resolve never to be alone with him. Tess frowned. But he'd kissed her in the presence of nearly a hundred party guests. What would stop him from trying the same in the dimly lit surroundings of a restaurant?

She groaned and sat down on a weathered marble bench. "What am I doing?" she murmured, rubbing her forehead with her fingers. "This is a dangerous game you're playing, Tess Ryan. And if you're not careful, you're going to lose your heart to him the same way Lucy did."

"YOU HAVE A DATE, don't you!"

Tess glanced over her shoulder at Lucy who was sprawled on Tess's bed, munching on a bag of cheese doodles. Lucy was dressed in a gorgeous silk robe, her long dark hair piled on top of her head, still damp from the one-hour bubble bath she'd just enjoyed.

"It's a business dinner," Tess said as she flipped through the appropriate dresses in her closet. She was drawn to a black jersey knit with sheer fabric over the arms and chest. Simple and slightly sexy, just enough to capture Drew's interest without shouting "seduce me."

"You're wearing eye shadow," Lucy commented as she nibbled on a doodle. "You never wear eye shadow for a business dinner. And if I'm not mistaken, that's my perfume in your hair."

Tess sighed. "All right. It's a little more than a business dinner."

"Who's the guy?" Lucy asked, rolling over on her stomach to watch Tess dress. "Is he cute?"

She shrugged and pulled the black dress off the hanger. "He's all right."

Tess couldn't recall telling a bigger lie in her life. Not even the time she convinced her mother that the red mark on her neck was a burn from her curling iron and not a love bite from Kevin Donnell.

"Well, that's not a very enthusiastic endorsement. What's wrong with him?"

"Nothing," Tess said, shaking her head. "It's just that…"

"What? You can talk to me, Tess. You always help me with my man problems. I could at least return the favor, offer my opinion. I *have* had a lot of experience, you know."

"All right," Tess said. "Maybe I could use your opinion. I have a hypothetical situation."

"You need to get shots to go on a date?"

"That's hypodermic, Luce. Hypothetical means pretend. Let's pretend that I've got a good friend. And she used to date this man, but things didn't work out. And then, I met this very same man and he asked me out."

"So you've horned in on your best friend's man?"

"No!" Tess cried. Basically that was the *Reader's Digest* condensed version, but it didn't do justice to the story. "Not exactly. I didn't mean to horn in. In fact, I didn't know who he was when I met him." She sat down on the bed and plucked at a loose thread on the hem of her dress. "I'm just worried about what will happen if my—friend finds out. Maybe I should tell her."

"Are you crazy?" Lucy cried, whacking Tess with the bag of cheese doodles. "I wouldn't tell her. It's not like you're dating him while she's still going out with him. He's fair game now."

"But don't you think that it's still a little devious? She's a very good friend."

"Girlfriends come and go," Lucy said flippantly. "But handsome men are what really count."

Tess groaned and jumped up from the bed. "That is exactly the attitude that has gotten you in so much trouble. You should have more girlfriends and fewer men in your life."

"So tell her, then," Lucy challenged. "See how good a friend she really is. She'll probably scratch your eyes out."

Just then, the phone rang and Lucy rolled over to pick it up. But Tess snatched the receiver out of her hand. If Drew had managed to track her down at the Duvelle party, she wouldn't put it past him to uncover her home phone number. "Hello?"

The male voice on the other end asked for Lucy and she turned the phone over to her sister. "It's a man," she said.

"Ooo, goody," Lucy said with a satisfied smile.

Tess continued to dress, listening halfheartedly to Lucy's animated phone conversation. Why couldn't she master the art of sparkling and witty conversation? Lucy could talk to a slab of marble and still find something interesting to say. Hell, she could go so far as to make the marble look like a brilliant conversationalist, as well.

"All right," Lucy said. "I'll meet you in an hour at Bistro Boulet."

Tess spun around and gaped at her sister. "Bistro Boulet? You're going to Bistro Boulet? But I'm going to Bistro Boulet!"

Lucy nodded as she set the phone back on the bedside table. "I know. That's what made me think of it. That was Serge. He's a furniture designer I met last year in

Lake Como. He's in town and wants to take me to dinner. I'm supposed to meet him at Boulet's at eight.''

But Tess was supposed to meet Drew at eight! Oh, Lord, what would she do now? She couldn't just stand him up, could she? If she arrived on time, she'd risk running into Lucy and her date. Maybe she could call Drew and change their plans. Tess cursed silently. He'd mentioned that he was coming directly from a business meeting and she didn't have a clue how to get hold of him.

"Eight?" Tess said, keeping her voice calm and even. "Do you really think you can be ready by eight? Maybe you should call him back and meet him at eight-thirty."

Lucy pushed up from the bed. "It's only Serge. He's just a friend. Hey, I have a great idea. Why don't we double-date. You're not so keen on your man, and my date barely speaks English. Why don't you join us at Boulet's?"

Tess wriggled into her dress then fumbled with the zipper in the back. "I—I don't think so, Luce."

Right now, all Tess could think about was the impending disaster. She could picture it, Lucy throwing a hissy fit in the middle of the restaurant. Plates flying across the room, insults hurled right along with sharp eating utensils. As she hurriedly slipped into her shoes, Tess grabbed her bag from the dresser. "I'm late," she said. "I have to go."

"Are you sure you don't want to double?" Lucy called.

"Not a chance," Tess muttered as she rushed out of the room and ran down the stairs. First, she'd need to avert another catastrophe. And then, she'd have to seriously reconsider her little plan to make Drew Wyatt fall in love with her. After all, the more time she spent with the man, the greater the opportunity for another disaster like this one. Though Lucy might be pleased that Tess had taken up her cause, she wondered if it might be going just a little too far for the sake of closure.

Maybe it would be best to put Drew Wyatt behind her for good. Then she'd convince Lucy to close the book on her own relationship with the man. And everything would finally get back to normal. Or as normal as life ever got living with Lucy Ryan Courault Battenfield Oleska.

4

TESS PEERED OUT from behind the front bumper of her Toyota, scanning the parking lot for Andrew Wyatt's black sedan. She had her plan down pat. If Lucy showed up first, she would dive for the shadows. And if Drew arrived first, she would dart out and waylay him before Lucy strolled in with Serge. It paid to have a plan, even if it changed by the minute. Still, Tess wasn't sure what she was going to do if they arrived at the same time…except maybe crawl under the car and pray for her dear life.

"This is getting out of hand," she murmured in disgust. "I should just step back and let it all happen. That would be the smart thing to do, Tess. Just let it blow up right here and now."

But like so many other instances in her life, she thought nothing of *her* wants and needs and only of Lucy's feelings. And though she wasn't exactly sure what she felt for Drew Wyatt, he didn't deserve to be humiliated in public.

But what did he deserve? Maybe her earlier instinct was right. Maybe a dose of his own medicine was exactly what he needed. Her sister would find closure and Drew might find himself a conscience. But did she really have what it took to coldly manipulate a man like Drew? Or was she simply trying to find an excuse to spend a little more time with him?

She had to admit, she was flattered by the attention he'd shown her. And she wanted to believe the attraction was genuine. Drew did seem to be a bit obsessed with her and that certainly was more interest than any other man had shown her in the past few years. One crook of her little finger might be all it took to draw him in.

Tess sighed. If she really wanted to hurt Drew, why was she doing everything in her power to protect him from Lucy? After all, he *was* the bad guy in this romantic triangle. But was she the woman who was going to make him pay? Or would she end up paying the price in the end? Tess cursed silently. If only she could sort out her confusion, then maybe she'd know what to do.

Footsteps sounded behind her and Tess scurried around to the other side of the car. She held her breath, and risked a look over the hood. Her heart lurched as she saw Drew stride past her with his sexy, loose-limbed gait. He wore an impeccably tailored business suit and a starched white shirt that contrasted starkly with his tanned face.

The night breeze ruffled his dark hair, softening his profile in the dim light of the streetlamps. Once again, she was struck by his arresting features, the chiseled jaw, the strong mouth, the straight nose. He had no right to be so handsome. And she had no business finding him so attractive. For a moment, she thought about letting him go, about turning around and walking away, leaving him to Lucy's histrionics.

Drew was just another in a long line of men that had dumped her sister. And though he might have led Lucy to believe they shared something more than a passing fling, Lucy did have a tendency to imagine a blissful future with every man she dated, no matter how unsuitable. "Stop making excuses for the man, Tess," she muttered to herself. "Good grief, you sound as if you're head over heels in love with him."

Tess winced inwardly. She couldn't fall in love with him! But in all honesty, she wasn't sure what she felt. There were moments when he made her believe she was the most beautiful, desirable woman in the world, moments when she could imagine them sharing something very special. And there were other times when she couldn't trust a single word he said, when she wanted to turn and run from his charming ways.

Now was not the time to examine her emotional state! Tess hurried out from behind her car and sprinted after Drew. She'd worry about the truth later. As she approached the front entrance to the restaurant, Tess glanced down the street. Her breath froze as she saw Lucy and her date converging on the very same spot. Panicked, she picked up her pace, determined to reach Drew before Lucy did.

She caught up with him in the foyer where he was carrying on a quiet conversation with the maître d'. With a move worthy of a NFL linebacker, Tess had just enough time to shove him into a dimly lit coatroom, her actions causing quite a stir among the five other patrons waiting. If she really expected to make him fall for her, she'd have to start sometime. And now was as good a time as any.

"What the—" Drew spun around then blinked in surprise. "Tess? What's going on?"

She glanced over her shoulder once, then yanked him deeper into the shadows when she noticed Lucy entering just a few feet away. She released her grip on his lapels and smiled wanly. "I've been waiting for you," she said in a whisper that sounded more winded than sexy.

"We were supposed to meet here at eight," he said, confusion marring his forehead. "I'm not late, am I?"

"Oh, no, you're not late."

"Is everything all right? You look a little...flushed."

At least she didn't look pale anymore. Her nightly encounter with the can of mineral spirits had finally done the trick. Tess deftly turned him around so his broad back faced the door, hiding her own body. "I—I'm just so happy to see you. So...excited." With that, she slipped her arms around his neck and drew him into the far corner of the alcove, far away from the prying eyes of the other customers and her sister, Lucy.

Drew stared down at her, his eyebrow arched. "Tess? What are you up to?"

She twisted his silk tie between her fingers and counted the seconds, hoping that Lucy and her date would be seated quickly. Lucy never had a problem getting a table in a restaurant. She just batted her eyes and smiled and maître d's and waiters automatically did her bidding, willing to trade a pretty smile for a large tip. "I'm really not hungry. Maybe we should get out of here," Tess murmured suggestively.

A lazy smile curled the corners of his lips. "You want to leave? Before we eat?"

Tess nodded, her heart beating so loudly she was sure he could hear it, her gaze captivated by his mouth. She could kiss him, she mused. She could pull him closer and plant one right on those perfectly chiseled lips of his. And better yet, she could write off the entire encounter as part of her plan to make him pay.

But instinct told her that once her lips touched his, she'd lose control. Just thinking about a kiss had muddled her brain and caused her pulse to pound. The actual kiss might render her completely senseless, incapable of rational thought.

He was probably an outstanding kisser. After all, lips

like his didn't come along every day. And what harm could one little kiss do? One quick, chaste meeting of two—Tess swallowed hard, dragging her eyes away from his mouth. "I—I want to leave. Now."

She said the last in a soft whisper, not to deliberately tempt him, but because she'd somehow lost her ability to breathe. Right now, she had to get both of them out of the restaurant without further embarrassment. If Drew thought something more intimate awaited them, then so be it. She'd deal with one problem at a time.

Drew grabbed her hand and they made their way to the front door. Tess couldn't help noticing the curious looks directed their way, the hidden whispers. Mortification slowly seeped through her as she realized what the other patrons were thinking. She and Drew had just been locked in a seemingly passionate embrace and now they were hurrying for the door, a sex-starved hussy and a handsome businessman.

When they reached the street, Drew casually slipped his arm around her waist. An unbidden thrill shot through Tess's body and her knees wobbled. Such a casual gesture, yet such a strong reaction. What would happen to her when he touched her with purpose? Would she keel over and lose consciousness, or become so addled she wouldn't be able to function?

Tess stumbled and he pulled her closer, the warmth of his body seeping through the soft fabric of her dress. She instinctively leaned into his body, like a kitten curling toward a spot of sunlight. But then she yanked herself back when all the wrong reactions raced through her.

This was a slippery slope she'd chosen, for with every step toward her goal, she found her resolve sliding back two. Why was he so hard to resist? He wasn't *that* charming...or handsome...or intelligent. If she could just remember who he was and what he'd done, her plan might have a chance to succeed. A slim, microscopic, subatomic particle-size chance.

"So where do you want to go?" he asked, splaying his fingers across her waist when they reached her car. He gently backed her up against the driver's-side door and bent close, responding to her fumbling and bumbling actions in the coatroom now that they were alone. "Your place or mine?"

Tess groaned inwardly, her gaze drawn to his mouth again. He was going to kiss her now, she just knew it! And it was all her fault. She steeled herself against the unwelcome flood of desire that she knew would come, then resigned herself to her fate by closing her eyes and tipping her mouth up. She waited and waited for his lips to touch hers, thinking of stubbed toes and needle pricks and dental surgery, anything painful enough to take her mind off the coming pleasure. She waited for the current of electricity to shoot through her body and for all her senses to go numb. But it never came.

Slowly, she opened her eyes to find him staring down at her, a crooked grin quirking his lips. "Are you sure you're all right, Tess? You're acting a little strange."

She drew in a sharp breath and cleared her throat. "Of course. I—I just thought you wanted to kiss me, that's all."

He drew a finger along her jawline and chuckled softly. "I *do* want to kiss you. I can't recall ever wanting to kiss a woman quite so much."

"Then what are you waiting for?" she asked, her breath coming in short, quick gasps. "Let's just get it over with."

He leaned closer, his mouth hovering over hers, his breath warm on her lips. "When I kiss you, Tess, it's not going to be in some dark parking lot. And it's not going to be over quickly. It's going to be long and sweet and it's something you'll want to go on and on and on. So, I'll choose the time and place, if that's all right with you.''

A tiny sigh slipped from her lips. ''Oh—that's fine,'' she said, her voice wavering. A long, lingering kiss sounded incredibly tempting...tantalizing...and—good grief! And potentially disastrous! Maybe it was time to abandon this ridiculous plan and cut her losses instead. After all, if she couldn't even get him to kiss her on demand, how did she expect to make him fall head over heels for her?

She needed to be the one in control and, right now, from what she could tell, Drew was the one behind the wheel. As for Tess, she hadn't even made it into the back seat for this wild ride. No, she felt as if she were being dragged behind the car by her hormones.

Every element in her plan rested on getting him to fall in love with her. If she couldn't accomplish that, she'd never be able to dump him. And if she fell in love with him first, she risked everything going awry. In the worst-case scenario, he'd be the one to dump her, as quickly as he'd dumped Lucy.

So why was that risk beginning to sound more and more tolerable? Perhaps it was the rewards—the kissing, the touching, the sweet words—everything that Lucy had found so irresistible.

Lucy. The more she got to know Drew, the more she believed that Lucy had been mistaken. He wasn't just some shallow guy on the make, the type of guy who'd deliberately break a girl's heart. There were so many inconsistencies in Lucy's view of Andrew Wyatt. Tess drew a long breath. Or was she imagining doubts where there were none, rationalizing her growing feelings by turning

Lucy into a certifiable flake and a merciless manhunter? And turning Drew into a paragon of manhood.

She forced a bright smile. "So, where are we going to go to eat?"

Drew frowned, taken aback and openly baffled by her mercurial shifts in mood. "Eat? I thought you wanted to leave."

"I did. But I'm still hungry. Starved, in fact. What do you think? Pizza? Chinese. There's a Polynesian place around the block." A noisy, crowded restaurant. A place where the conversation couldn't become too intimate, where they couldn't sit too close. A place where she could pass their one and only "date" in relative safety, then rush home to regroup.

"All right," Drew with a resigned shrug. "If you want Polynesian, Tess, we'll eat Polynesian."

"And I'll drive my own car," she added. "You can follow me."

"This is like no date I've ever been on," Drew muttered as he headed toward his car. "A surprise every minute."

Tess watched him walk away, then collapsed against the side of the car, groaning softly. "No more surprises," she said. "After tonight, Drew Wyatt will be out of my life for good!"

THE KING KAMANIMANI South Seas Tiki Palace and Cocktail Lounge wasn't exactly in the same class as Bistro Boulet, but Drew didn't seem to mind. Tess suspected that he was happy as long as she appeared happy, and she did her best to look that way. Right now, King Kamanimani's was the perfect place to put some distance between Drew and herself.

After they'd been seated in a rustic booth with a palm-frond roof, Drew ordered a bottle of wine, only to learn from the pudgy waitress in the grass skirt that the Tiki Palace's wine list consisted of a red and a white, both of unknown origin. The server also informed him that the wine didn't come in bottles, but right out of a cool little plastic bag. She offered a flaming fruit-and-rum special in a coconut shell instead. Drew opted for a beer, while Tess ordered the special.

The waitress returned a few minutes later to an uncomfortable silence between them, setting their drinks on the table and taking their order while making minor adjustments to her coconut bra. Drew told her to take her time with the food, but as Tess took in the family atmosphere of the Tiki Palace, she didn't think there'd be much opportunity to linger. All the better.

She reached for her drink, then noticed it was still on fire. With a soft cry, she blew at it and beat it with her napkin. Once the fire had been extinguished, Tess took a long swallow of the sweet concoction, the elaborate fruit decorations poking at her nose.

"Do you come here often?" Drew asked with a wry smile.

She put down her nearly empty coconut shell and licked her lips. "Why?"

"Because this is the last place I'd expect to find a woman like you," he said softly. "I don't associate you with grass skirts and fruity drinks."

"I rented this place once for a children's birthday party," Tess explained. "It has such a kitschy atmosphere. Kids love it." A smile twitched at her lips. "I had a headache for three days afterward." She pointed up to the speaker above their head. "From the drums."

Drew chuckled. "I didn't notice them until now. So, do you like children?"

"Oh, I love children," Tess replied dryly. "One or two at a time. Quiet, polite children without something sticky in their hands. I don't do kids' parties anymore."

Drew reached out and grabbed her hand, lacing his fingers through hers. Her first impulse was to pull away, but then she realized that she didn't want to. She liked the feel of his warm fingers wrapped around hers. And it was an innocent enough gesture, one that didn't necessarily lead to passion. Age-old advice from her stepmother flitted through her mind. The best way to cool a man's passion is to keep your feet on the floor and all your buttons buttoned, Rona had advised. They all want the same thing and it's your job to see that they don't get it. Too bad Lucy hadn't followed that advice. If she had, maybe Tess wouldn't be in the middle of this mess.

"I've always wanted two kids," he teased, studying her carefully painted nails. "Or maybe three. What do you think about three children?"

Tess swallowed hard. This was not a proper subject for a first date! Why did he persist in tormenting her? Was he joking or serious? A hot blush worked its way up her cheeks. "I—I don't think we should be talking about our—any children. After all, we barely know each other."

He shrugged, then removed his hand from hers, leaned back and unknotted his silk tie. "Maybe you're right. It is too early to talk about marriage. We should save that for the second or third date. So, what do we talk about on our first date? Tell me."

"You should know," she said, squirming against the vinyl booth and plucking at the paper lei the hostess had placed around her neck. "I'm sure you've had plenty of first dates."

"Not lately." He leaned closer and covered her fingers with his once more. "In fact, I'll tell you a little secret if you promise not to pass it around. I haven't had a date in months.''

"Liar," she said, snatching her hand away.

His eyebrow arched. "You don't believe me?"

"I'm not sure I believe anything you say. I think you like to make me…confused. Keep me off balance."

"What are you confused about? I've been perfectly honest with you. Ask me anything and I'll tell you the truth."

Tess rearranged the flatware in front of her and waved to the waitress for another flaming-rum punch. "Anything? And you'll tell me the absolute truth."

Drew held up his hand as a pledge. "The truth and nothing but the truth, so help me King Kamanimani."

"All right. Who was the last woman you dated?"

"That would be Cassandra Wentland," he answered promptly.

Tess frowned. She didn't care for that answer. The truth and nothing but the truth would have produced an entirely different name—her sister's! Unless he'd managed to date someone after Lucy and before he met her, the two-timing cad. "When?"

"When did I date her? I don't know. Maybe six or seven months ago. It was just one date. Then I had to leave for Tokyo and she moved on to someone more attentive. Someone residing in the same hemisphere."

"All right. When was the last time you told a woman you loved her?"

"Last month." He grinned. "I called my mother. It was her birthday. I got emotional. I lost my head. What can I say? Please, don't be jealous."

She frowned. "I mean other than a relative. When was the last time you told a woman you were involved with that you loved her?"

He considered her question for a long moment and she wondered if he was making up another lie. "Sarah McKellar," he finally replied. "I was a junior in high school and she was the most beautiful girl I'd ever seen. Until I met you, that is. She was going with my best friend and I thought if I'd only be honest with her, she'd dump him and go out with me."

"And did she?"

"Nah. She told my buddy and he got a bunch of guys together and they beat me up. And that was the last time I ever said it. You don't have brothers, do you?"

Tess laughed nervously. She had braced herself for the truth, for him to admit to his relationship with her sister. And she was prepared to tear into him, to give him a good-size piece of her mind. But he made no mention of loving Lucy. And worse yet, he turned his answer into a subtle insinuation that he might someday love her.

So he hadn't said those three little words to her sister. And he had no logical motive to lie about this to Tess. According to his version of the story, they hadn't even dated. But Lucy wasn't a forgettable woman. When a man dated her, he remembered her, sometimes for years and years afterward.

She pressed her fingers into her temples and tried to rub away the confusion that assaulted her mind. Who was she supposed to believe? This fascinating man who could set her blood afire with just one devastating smile and a few offhand words. Or her overly emotional, man-crazy sister. What if Lucy had lied? Or exaggerated their relationship just a bit? That would change everything. Drew would be the victim in this whole mess, the victim of both Lucy's imagination and her attempts at vengeance.

But they'd spent weekends together and there was that trip to Maui! And the gifts. How could her sister have imagined those? Tess took a sip of her fresh drink and glanced around the room. He was a pathological liar. That was the only explanation. The rum was beginning to make her think much more clearly.

Her gaze darted over at him only to catch him watching her. Tess forced a weak smile. "I—I hope they bring our food soon. I'm really hungry."

"Now it's my turn," Drew said. "The truth and nothing but the truth."

"Maybe we should change the subject. How about work? Why don't you tell me the truth about your job?"

Drew picked up his beer and took a long sip. "From my love life to my work. That's an interesting shift, Tess. How come we never talk about you? If I were a suspicious man, I might think you were hiding something. A shady past. A husband you don't want me to know about."

"I talk about myself," Tess said, her voice defensive.

"You didn't answer my question about brothers. Do you have any?"

"No brothers," Tess said. "Now, about your work."

Looking exasperated with her evasions, he leaned back and shook his head wearily. "Well, there is something rather peculiar going on at work, now that you mention it. You remember the flat tires from the other night?"

Tess nodded. How could she possibly forget? That had been the first sign of trouble. "Of course. Did the police catch the vandals?"

"It wasn't vandals," Drew said. "In fact, I think I know who did it."

Tess was in the midst of gulping her rum punch when she drew in a sharp breath. Suddenly, her eyes began to water and a cough burst from her throat. With a frantic hand, she pounded on her chest, but the coughing wouldn't stop.

Drew quickly stood and patted her on the back and the waitress with the grass skirt rushed over and demanded to perform the Heimlich. Even the huge bartender with the machete in his belt came to the table and offered to give her a good shake. But Tess waved them away and continued to cough. By now, tears were streaming down her face, her nose was running and her throat burned.

Finally, wheezing and sniffling, she regained control. She wiped her eyes with her napkin and took a careful sip of water. "I—I'm sorry. It just went down the wrong way. I'll be all right. Please, go on."

"Go on?"

"Yes," Tess said, anxious to hear exactly what Drew had to say. "Tell me about the vandals."

Drew stared at her a long moment with a baffled look. "It wasn't vandals," he repeated.

"H-how do you know?"

"Well, I didn't until yesterday. Until the policewoman showed up."

Tess gasped. "You—you called the police?"

"Yes. And when a policewoman showed up at my office, I thought she was there to get my statement. Until she ripped off her blouse and started wiggling her backside."

This time, Tess snatched up her napkin and coughed into it. Her eyes began to water again and she moaned softly. "I don't understand. A policewoman took off her—"

"She took it all off. And in front of some very important clients. And she wasn't a real policewoman, she was a stripper. But I finally figured out what this was all about. I know who's behind it. In fact, I've got my business manager on the case. He's hired a private investigator."

"A—a private investigator?" Tess asked, her heart

slamming in her chest. First the police, then a private detective. Oh, God, it was all over now. Lucy had gone too far hiring a stripper! One trick too many had pushed Drew to the edge. It wouldn't be long before his investigator found out the truth. Maybe Drew already knew. Tess swallowed hard. She should just confess and get it over with, practice a little damage control and salvage what she could. "What did this investigator find?"

"Nothing yet," Drew replied. "But Sam Lubich is behind it. I'd be willing to stake my recently tarnished reputation on it."

A sigh of relief escaped her tightly pursed lips and she sank back into the booth. "Sam Lubich?"

"Lubich and Roth Architects. He's a competitor. A real unscrupulous businessman. We're bidding against each other on the new civic center project. He's out to embarrass me in front of the committee. But once I get the proof I need, he'll be finished. No one will want to hire him."

"You're going to—to ruin him?"

Drew shook his head. "He'll ruin himself. And I'll be there to applaud."

Tess grabbed her coconut and drained it. She wasn't sure whether she should be pleased or concerned. He hadn't connected Lucy with all the trickery. Not yet. Now if she could only get Lucy to stop, maybe she might be able to contain the mess she'd created. But what about poor Mr. Lubich, *innocent* Mr. Lubich?

Could she really hope to control the situation when so many people were involved? At first it had been the three of them, but now there was Lubich and the investigator and Drew's business manager. She couldn't possibly keep track of people she didn't even know.

"Oh, look," Tess said in a bright voice. "Here come our pupu platters. I'm starved." For now, food would provide the perfect alternative to conversation. And while she ate, she could contemplate the next disaster that she was sure awaited her.

FOR DREW, the food arrived far too soon. Whenever he asked Tess a question, he found her with a mouthful of pupu. She'd nod and smile and deftly avoid answering in any detail, leaving him with the distinct impression that she was hiding something from him. He bided his time, but when she finished one selection, she quickly grabbed another until she'd eaten nearly half the platter on her own.

He had to admire her appetite, but he figured if he continued his attempts, she'd eat so much he'd have to carry her out of King Kamanimani's on a stretcher. She finally stopped when the waitress brought the check and picked up the empty platter.

"Anything else?" the server asked, glancing at Drew, then at Tess.

Tess shook her head and held up her hand. "No," she said with her mouth full. "Nothing else. We're done. Thanks." She snatched up her napkin and dabbed at her lips, then glanced over at the check. He made no move to pick it up. The hell if he was going to let this bizarre excuse for a date end before it had even started. He wanted to get to know Tess Ryan better and that's what he was intent on accomplishing.

"Why are you in such a hurry?" he asked, studying her shrewdly, drawing the check toward him with his finger. "Are you that anxious to leave?" He deserved at least an attempt at interesting conversation. All he got was a guilty shrug.

"I have an early appointment tomorrow," Tess said. "I should be going."

"Tess, it's barely nine o'clock. You plan parties that start later than this. Come on. Am I that boring?"

"Nine o'clock? It—it seemed like at least midnight."

"Answer my question."

Tess sighed. "No," she snapped. "You're not boring. I'm sure you're a very nice man, Drew, but—"

"But what? The truth and nothing but the truth, Tess."

She began slowly, hesitantly. "The truth is, I had a good time tonight. I didn't want to. I tried not to, but I did."

"Then we can go out again?"

She sighed. "Maybe. Sometime."

His jaw tightened and he fought a frustrated impulse to drag her over the table and kiss her until she started behaving like the Tess he thought he knew. "You admitted you enjoy my company. You find me attractive. Let's move on to my personal habits. I don't have any that offend you, do I?"

She blinked in surprise. "No. Not that I can think of."

He pulled his wallet from his jacket and tossed a few bills on the table, then reached across and grabbed her hand. "Come on. Let's get out of here."

He pulled her toward the door, and when they reached the street he stopped and turned her to face him. Without any warning, he brought his mouth down on hers in a startling and surprisingly passionate kiss, a kiss he'd promised would be so much more.

Drew's aggravation slowly dissolved beneath the sweet taste of her lips. All this talk was getting him nowhere. It was time for action, quick and decisive. His tongue touched hers and a warm flood of desire pumped through his body, pooling in his lap.

At first, she didn't respond and he waited for her to pull away. But then, she softened in his arms and leaned into his body, her mouth pliant against his. He'd never expected it to be quite so perfect, especially not the first time, but it was. She was made for his arms, every curve of her body fitting easily against his. His mind flashed to an image of the two of them naked, of Tess lying on top of him and below him, her arms wrapped around him.

A low groan rumbled in his throat and he pulled back, pushing aside his runaway fantasies. Her eyes were closed and her mouth turned up to his. So much for waiting for the right moment, Drew thought. He'd have preferred to kiss her someplace more romantic, but he was starting to realize that a guy had to grab his chances when he could with Tess Ryan.

She slowly opened her eyes, her gaze resting on his mouth. He tried to resist, but he couldn't stop himself from kissing her again. His hands slid around her waist, then over her hips, and he drew her against him. But this time, she pulled away, leaving him aching for more.

"Thank you for dinner," Tess murmured. "I had a lovely time."

He smiled and let his fingers tangle with hers. "We will have to do it again," Drew said, his eyes skimming over her flushed features. "Soon." Was it desire he saw there, or just the aftereffects of too much rum?

"Yes, soon," she said in a tone that was less than convincing.

He still couldn't tell if she really meant what she said or if she was simply placating him. After what had happened tonight, he wasn't sure what was going on in Tess's head. She certainly wasn't the woman he'd met that night at the art museum, the woman who'd danced and laughed with him in the alley. Nor was she the woman who'd dragged him into the coatroom at Bistro Boulet an hour ago. The longer he knew Tess Ryan, the odder her behavior became.

He flipped back through their time together and tried to pinpoint when everything had turned from stimulating to downright strange. He kept coming back to the flat tires on his car. But how could four flat tires alter her feelings for him? Or completely change her personality?

"I better go now," Tess said, interrupting his thoughts.

He nodded, resigned to her decision. "Call me."

She looked up and frowned. "Call *you?*"

"Yes," he said, as if his request was perfectly reasonable. "The next time you'd like to go out, call me."

Tess blinked, clearly surprised by his suggestion. "But—but, I—"

Drew raked his hands through his hair and sighed in exasperation. "The ball's in your court, Tess. You make the next move—if there's going to be a next move."

"And what if there isn't?" she asked.

He ground his teeth. "Then that's up to you. I can handle rejection as well as the next guy. But I think we have something special here. And I also think you like me a lot more than you're willing to admit."

She sniffed disdainfully. "You have a rather high opinion of yourself, Drew Wyatt."

"No, I have good intuition. I'm not sure why you're fighting this. Maybe you've been hurt badly in the past and you're spooked. Maybe you're too absorbed in your career to make time for a social life. Or maybe you're just loony. To be honest, I don't need any explanations. I just hope that you don't blow the best thing that's happened to either one of us in a very long time."

Tess laughed nervously. He knew he sounded arrogant, but he didn't care. There was nothing left to lose. Charm hadn't worked, nor had honesty. Maybe it was time to get a little indignant.

"You're the best thing that's ever happened to me?" she asked.

"I could be," Drew said, "if you'd give me half a chance." He leaned closer, his mouth nearly touching hers. This time, she didn't close her eyes and wait. Instead, she stared back at him, challenging him to kiss her again. But he wasn't about to give her the pleasure or the satisfaction.

"I think I need to get up early tomorrow, too," he murmured. "*I* better be going." With that, Drew turned on his heel and walked toward his car, leaving Tess standing alone in front of the Tiki Palace, her silhouette illuminated by the flaming torches that flanked the front door.

"Don't think because you're walking away from me it changes my feelings for you," she shouted.

"Then you admit you have feelings for me?" he called, not bothering to look back.

"I might not call," she replied. "So don't hold your breath."

Drew chuckled to himself and kept walking. One of these days, he'd figure Tess Ryan out. But until then, she sure was an interesting puzzle. A stubborn, exasperating, desirable puzzle. But then, Drew Wyatt had always loved a good puzzle.

5

THE WEATHER HAD TURNED warm in Atlanta and the midday breeze fluttered the lace curtains in Tess's bedroom. She stretched sinuously and rolled over in bed, pulling her pillow against her chest. The scent of flowering trees hung in the air and she closed her eyes and drew a deep breath.

But instead of the usual cheery springtime images—birds and bees and bunnies—a handsome face invaded her thoughts, with arresting blue eyes and a wicked smile. Tess moaned into her pillow. It had been nearly a week since she had pupu with Drew and she still couldn't seem to put him out of her mind.

Every time the phone rang at work, she wondered if he was on the other end of the line. She looked for him on the street and at parties she had planned, hoping that they might run into each other by chance. She had even found herself wishing that Lucy would pull another one of her stunts so that Tess could ride to the rescue.

But she couldn't bring herself to call him, even though that's exactly what she wanted to do. If she called Drew, it would be tantamount to admitting that she was falling in love with him. And loving Drew Wyatt would be the worst of all possible problems.

If there was one ray of hope in her miserable week it was that Lucy had neatly put Drew out of her mind. She'd been well occupied with showing her fussy furniture designer around Atlanta. Tess hadn't heard her mention the name Andrew Wyatt since his arrival, though she dearly hoped that wasn't because Lucy was falling in love with Serge.

"Maybe this is the end of it," Tess said as she sat up in bed. "Or maybe it's just a new beginning." Neither thought provided any comfort or relief. Instead, the words rang hollowly in her mind and a stab of regret pierced her heart. She thought back to the moment that she had met Andrew Wyatt, to a time when he wasn't Lucy's ex but simply a charming stranger in a tuxedo.

Was it her destiny in life to meet an endless string of unsuitable men? With a muttered oath, Tess rolled out of bed and grabbed her robe. It wouldn't do to dwell on what might have been. Work would occupy her mind and erase any residual thoughts of Drew. As she padded through the house toward the kitchen, she deliberately attempted to fix her mind on the workday ahead. But the catering menu for the Atlanta Symphony reception dissolved in her head as soon as she walked into the breakfast room.

Her sister was bent over a pile of shattered china, the remains of her stepmother's favorite Villeroy and Boch. As soon as she heard Tess, Lucy dropped the dustpan and hand broom and stood up. "Good," she said. "I'm glad you're finally awake. Did the noise bother you?"

Tess gaped at the mess and shook her head. "Luce, what happened here? What did you do to Rona's china?"

Her sister glanced at the broken dishes with a dismissive sniff. "I've always hated that china. It's so gaudy. Who can face all those fruits and vegetables lurking beneath your food?"

"Did you purposely break those dishes?"

Lucy nodded. "I had a good reason! He was there. At Bistro Boulet. With another woman."

Tess slid into a chair a moment before her legs went

boneless. "Who was there?" she asked, knowing the answer. Lucy couldn't have seen them together, could she? Why hadn't she mentioned this sooner? And exactly what had she seen? Tess remembered that the majority of their time at the bistro had been spent in the coatroom.

"Andy! At the restaurant that night I was there with Serge. Mima Fredrikson called and told me that her sister was there, waiting for a table. Her sister is a volunteer at the art museum. Well, it was all the talk among the restaurant staff. Andy and this hussy were necking in the lobby and then they turned around and walked out, without eating dinner! Oh, I wish I'd run into him. If he thinks he can just turn those gorgeous brown eyes on a woman and—"

"Blue," Tess said, watching Lucy's tantrum as she picked up her coffee cup.

"What?"

The coffee burned Tess's throat and she winced at her careless words. "The sky. It's so blue today, isn't it?"

Lucy ignored her clumsy commentary on the weather and continued her rant. "Mima's sister said she was really a hag though. I wish I'd run into him! I would have showed him just how much I'm over him. I am *so* over him."

"A hag?" Tess asked. "A *hag?*" Indignation overcame her bruised ego and she ground her teeth. She had looked good that night! Her hair had managed to hold a curl and the dress she'd worn was one of her favorites, a style that de-emphasized all her major figure flaws. She'd even done a passable job on her makeup. All that to be reduced to a description usually reserved for crones and witches.

"Actually, Mima said she was just kind of slutty. You know, hanging all over him. Anyway, I got even."

"Even?"

Lucy grinned and slid into the car across from Tess. "Yeah. Big time. Remember how I said I wanted to dye his dog green."

Tess groaned as her coffee cup clattered into its saucer. "You didn't do that, did you?"

"No," Lucy replied. She paused long enough for Tess to feel a small measure of relief, then continued. "I died him purple. Lavender, actually. A very pretty shade. Almost the same color as that cashmere shawl of yours. Lavender is very big this year. *A la dernière mode.*"

Tess buried her face in her hands and moaned. "Aw, Luce. I thought you were over him." She looked up at her sister. "How did you do it?"

A coy smile curled Lucy's lips. "I snuck into his place. I know the gate code and he always lets that dopey dog run around the yard during the day. The silly mutt just came right up to me and—"

Tess pushed her coffee cup back, then stood up. "What's the code?" she demanded.

"It's 2-5-9-0. What do you need to know the code for?"

"And the dog's name?" she asked as she strode to the kitchen door.

"Rufus," Lucy snapped. "Why do you need to know that, Tess? You're not going to turn me in, are you? If you rat me out, Tess, I'll never forgive you. I'll hate you for the rest of my life. You'll be—"

Tess blocked out the remainder of her sister's protests as she raced up the stairs to her room. "Here we go again," she muttered as she yanked her clothes on.

SHE EASILY FOUND Drew's house, recognizing the tall brick pillars that flanked the gated driveway—and the bush that still showed traces of white paint. She pulled the car to the curb, slammed on the brakes, then got out and punched in the security code that Lucy had given her.

Lucy. Once again her sister had thrown both their lives into chaos. At first, Tess had wondered how any man could have such a hold over a woman. But she had to admit that Drew Wyatt held an undeniable fascination. She could hardly blame Lucy for her obsessive behavior. Over the past week, Tess had indulged in a few obsessions of her own, like daydreaming about his smile, fantasizing about his body, wondering about the true depth of his desire. And reliving their kisses, again and again, until her head spun and her pulse quickened.

Tess moaned softly and forced herself to imagine Lucy and Drew together. Lately, it was the only thing that stopped the fantasies. Still, no matter how she composed the image, she couldn't picture the two of them in each other's arms. They just didn't fit. Drew was such a no-nonsense kind of guy. And Lucy was the poster girl for nonsense. What could they possibly have in common? What *had* they possibly had in common?

"Maybe they didn't do much talking, Tess," she said as she shoved the gate open. A raucous bark shocked her into the present and she quickly pulled the gate shut again, putting solid iron bars between her and Drew's slavering dog.

The pooch came bounding out from behind a row of bushes, and though she'd been warned, the sight of Rufus took Tess by surprise. It was hard for a bright lavender dog to look ferocious and threatening. In fact, he looked no more frightening than one of the huge stuffed animals that Tess had kept on her bed when she was a teenager.

Rufus stood on the other side of the iron gate, his crooked tail flopping back and forth, his pink tongue lolling out of his mouth and dripping with drool. He probably hadn't ever been a particularly cute dog, not even as a puppy. But he looked even worse dyed a stylish shade of purple.

Tess bent down and held out her hand between the bars of the gate. The dog licked her fingers enthusiastically. "Oh, Lucy," she cried. "What have you done to this poor animal?" She tried to imagine some cruelty to Rufus, but in all honesty, the dog seemed to enjoy his new look. He pranced back and forth behind the fence, head held high, as he waited for her to come inside and play with him.

"How am I going to explain this one away?" she murmured, punching in the security code again. "He's going to know who did this. He's going to know it's not that Lubich guy and he'll go right to Lucy. And she'll probably tell him how I'm involved, how I suggested this whole thing, and he'll find out we're sisters and then—"

Tess pushed the gate open and Rufus came bounding out, sniffing her feet and legs before sitting down with a satisfied "Woof!" She stared at him for a long moment, then glanced at her watch. If she moved quickly, she'd have just enough time to fix Lucy's latest fiasco and get back before Drew found his dog missing.

She grabbed Rufus's collar and spoke to him softly. "Come on, buddy. You and I are going for a little ride." As soon as Rufus caught sight of her car, he ran over to the driver's-side door and waited, his tail sweeping the ground. Tess let him in and he settled himself on the passenger seat. She reached over and secured the seat belt as best as she could, then smiled at the purple dog. "I want you to be a good dog now. No barking and stay in your seat. And try to control that drooling."

Mr. Randy's Hair Emporium was only a fifteen-minute drive from Drew's house. During their ride together, Rufus managed to wiggle out of the seat belt and explore the entire interior of Tess's Toyota. He barked at every truck that passed, howled at a police siren, threw up once in the back seat, then contented himself to sit on Tess's lap with his purple head hanging out her open window.

When Tess finally pulled up in front of Mr. Randy's, she was covered with both purple dog hair and dog saliva, and she smelled a little funky as well. Wincing at the odor, Tess opened the car door and gave Rufus a little push. But this time, he didn't want to move. In fact, Rufus was quite intent on staying right were he was.

"I'm not going to waste precious minutes trying to talk you out of this car," Tess said, wiggling out from beneath his paws. When she'd finally removed herself from the car, she reached in and grabbed hold of Rufus, then hefted him up into her arms. For such a wiry dog, he weighed a ton! And he smelled even worse at such close range.

Mr. Randy's receptionist watched, wide-eyed, as Tess struggled through the glass doors with the dog. She snapped her gum, then smiled. "Cool pooch!" she said. "I didn't know you had a dog."

"He's not mine." Tess noticed that the girl had a purple streak in her blond hair, the exact same shade as Rufus's. "What is that color you have in your hair?"

"Purple Passion," the receptionist explained. "It's a good color for Libras. Is your dog a Libra?"

"Does it come out?" Tess asked hopefully.

She snapped her gum and shook her head. "Nah, it's pretty permanent. Unless you put another color over it. Or bleach it out."

Tess groaned. "I need to see Mr. Randy. Tell him Tess Ryan is here and it's an emergency."

She found an inconspicuous spot in the reception area and ordered Rufus to lie down at her feet. To her surprise, he did as he was told, flopping down in a heap, his chin on his front paws.

A few minutes later, Mr. Randy appeared in an outfit that was the human equivalent of Rufus's purple coat. Mr. Randy was one of the best stylists in Atlanta, if you could get past his flamboyant wardrobe and his penchant for society-page gossip. A look of concern furrowed his forehead as he approached. "Tess, darling!" he called in the fake European accent he favored. "Nicole said it was an emergency."

He hurried over and began to run his hands through her mussed hair, studying it carefully and clucking his tongue. "Oh, this *is* an emergency. You were right to come. Mr. Randy will make it all better."

Tess suspected she looked as if she'd lived through a train wreck, but Rufus was her main concern. "Not me," she said, pushing his fluttering hands away. "It's him." She pointed to the purple dog and Rufus looked up.

Mr. Randy gasped and jumped back. "It's alive! It's alive!" he cried.

"Of course it's alive," Tess replied. "It's a dog."

Mr. Randy blinked, stunned. "I—I thought it was your coat." He bent over and peered at Rufus, then shook his head. "This is not a look I would recommend for a dog. Me, myself, I prefer a more…natural look. Brown or black."

"I know. Can you fix it? Can you make him look like a dog again?"

He sniffed, then reached out and ran his fingers through Rufus's coat. "He needs to go into more of the red tones, I think. Maybe with a few blond highlights. This would bring out his eyes. A shorter cut would make the hair move, give it more body. And we need to do a deep condition, darling. His hair is very dry. Has he been using hot rollers?''

Tess screamed out of sheer frustration. "He's a dog! He takes a bath with his tongue and he sleeps in the garden. If you showed him a hot roller, he'd probably bury it."

"But he *is* purple," Mr. Randy countered. "Someone has been doing his hair. And not very well, I might add."

"I—I know," she replied, trying to calm her impatience. "That was a little prank that someone pulled. I just need to get him back to normal—and fast. Can you help? Please, Mr. Randy? I'm desperate here. You're the only person I could trust with this."

Mr. Randy hitched his hands on his hips and gave her a haughty look. "Darling, when it comes to color, you know I am the best in Atlanta. You just leave it to me. When you see him next, he will be a whole new dog." He turned to Nicole. "Cancel my next two appointments, and when Mrs. Stillwell is finished under the dryer, have Duane comb her out."

With that, Mr. Randy patted his hip and whistled. To Tess's amazement, Rufus sprung to his feet and loped after the hairdresser, disappearing into the depths of the salon. Tess glanced at her watch. By her calculation, her hairdresser had less than four hours to turn Rufus from a purple pooch into a regular mutt. And she had exactly the same amount of time to formulate an explanation if Mr. Randy's magic didn't work.

Over the next two hours, Tess paced the reception area, flipped through countless magazines and carried on a baffling conversation with Nicole over the existence of extraterrestrials in the greater Atlanta area. She was about to violate the privacy of Mr. Randy's inner sanctum when the hairdresser came hurrying out.

To Tess's dismay, Rufus was nowhere to be seen. "What's wrong?" she asked. "Where's the dog? Is he all right?"

"Prepare yourself, darling. I think I've outdone myself!" He whistled softly and Rufus came running out from the rear of the salon. Tess's eyes went wide as she stared at the dog in amazement. He didn't look like a mutt anymore. He looked like a movie star!

"What did you do?" she cried.

"It was nothing," Mr. Randy replied with feigned humility.

"No! I mean, he looks better than he's supposed to. He's supposed to be…ugly. Kind of scruffy-looking. He's not even drooling anymore!"

"Scruffy is not a good look for him either," Randy said. "I saw into his soul and this is the dog I saw. Look at the depth of the color. I double highlighted it. And then I gave it a golden rinse so it would shine in the sun. I evened out the color on his ears, and look at his toes! Melinda gave him a little manicure!" He giggled and clapped his hands. "Isn't that cute?"

Tess could see she wasn't getting through to Mr. Randy. Rufus might as well have been purple again. Drew would notice something was up right away. But she didn't have time to make any more changes. Perhaps if she took Rufus home and tossed a little dirt on him, she might be able to tone down Mr. Randy's highlights. "How much do I owe you?" she asked.

Randy looked down at Rufus. "Four hundred fifty-seven," he said.

"Dollars?"

"No, rubles," Randy said. "Of course, dollars! Look at all I had to do for this poor dog. Beauty doesn't come cheap, darling."

Reluctantly, Tess made out a check for the amount plus a reasonable tip, then led Rufus out to the street. The dog glanced up at her and she could have sworn he was smirking. But then he wagged his tail and woofed softly and Tess was forced to smile.

"You do look pretty good," she said as she opened the car door. "And I'd venture to guess that you smell a whole lot better. Now, hop in and let's get you back home before your master misses you."

DREW POKED at his car stereo, scanning the Clapton disc for a song to put him in a good mood. The weather was warm and a sweet breeze poured through the windows as he sped toward home. Yet even with "Layla" blaring from the speakers, he still couldn't shake the restlessness that had plagued him day and night for the past week.

It had to be Tess. Business was good, the civic center bid was coming along well and Lubich hadn't pulled any of his slimy tricks in nearly a week. Even though Drew had tried to put Tess out of his head, she kept creeping back in at the oddest times. He turned the corner onto his street and slowed as he reached for the control to the gate.

But as he drove nearer, Drew noticed a woman standing in the middle of the driveway, peering into his front yard through the gate. He blinked, then frowned. Tess? Drew pulled off his sunglasses and squinted, sure that his eyes were playing tricks on him. But it was Tess's dark hair and slender figure that he saw, her tidy business suit and her sensible heels. And her incredible legs. As the car pulled up to the driveway, he noticed her Toyota parked on the other side of the street.

"It was your move, Tess," he murmured, smiling. "It sure took you long enough to make it." He parked the car, hopped out and quietly approached her. She seemed oblivious to his presence, her attention focused on something inside the fence.

"Tess?"

With a start and a tiny scream, she spun around. Her green eyes went wide and she shifted from foot to foot, glancing nervously over her shoulder into the yard and then back at him. "What are you doing here?" she asked.

"I live here," he said. "What are *you* doing here?"

"You live here," she repeated, nodding solemnly. "That's such a…coincidence. I—I was just driving through the neighborhood and I had a little car trouble and I—"

Drew wagged his finger at her. "And you're not telling me the truth, Tess," he said. "Give me your keys and I'll check out your car."

She reached in her jacket pocket and withdrew her keys, then thought better of it and snatched them back. "All right. Maybe I was curious."

"And maybe you wanted to see me again?"

"I thought you'd be at work for at least another few hours," she muttered. "I didn't think you'd be home early or I wouldn't have…stayed."

For all the bravado in her gaze, he still didn't believe her. There was something more in her demeanor, another truth she was trying to keep from him. Now what was she up to? "Since I'm home early and it's a beautiful April afternoon, why don't you come on in and I'll show you the house. Just to appease your curiosity. Then, if you're hungry, I'll make you some dinner. If you're not, you can go home."

"I can't," Tess said. "I've got to—"

Drew reached out and pressed his finger to her lips. "If you come in, I'll pretend that your car did break down. I'll even pretend to call the auto club for you."

He waited for her to smile the same way he waited for the sun to come out on a cloudy day. When she looked at him and the corners of her mouth lifted, warmth flooded his senses and he took her hand in his. "So, have you had these problems with your car before?" he asked. "It could be the timing belt. Or maybe the fuel pump. These foreign cars can be touchy."

He opened the gate and they walked through, leaving his car where he'd parked it. Rufus bounded up as they strolled toward the house, his tongue hanging out of his mouth. Drew bent down and gave the dog a pat on the head, then stepped back. It had to be his mood, the happiness he felt at finding Tess waiting at the gate, but he could swear Rufus looked different. In truth, the mutt actually looked…cute.

"What is it?" Tess asked.

Drew shook his head. "I don't know. Does he look a little…"

"A little what?" Tess snapped. "Hot? Happy? Skinny?"

"A little lavender? I mean, in the right light, his coat looks kind of…purple."

"Don't be silly," Tess said, laughing and linking her arm in his. She drew him down the driveway toward the house. "Dogs aren't purple. Who ever heard of a purple dog?"

Drew gave Rufus one last look, then shrugged and turned toward Tess. "You're right."

When they arrived at the front door, Drew ushered Tess inside. He stood behind her as she stared up at the cathedral ceiling in the foyer, her eyes caught by the narrow windows that gleamed high above them, the streams of light flooding warm wooden floors. Slowly, she moved toward the open staircase and skimmed her fingers over the carved newel post.

Drew had worked on the design for this house beginning the day he'd graduated from architecture school. It combined the simplicity of Frank Lloyd Wright with a cozy arts-and-crafts sensibility and a touch of Southern sprawl. Every detail had been painstakingly perfected, designed and redesigned until he was certain that he could live with it for a lifetime. But as he watched Tess take it all in, he realized that the house meant nothing to him. It was just a place to get out of the rain. The right woman turned it into a home, filled it with warmth and happiness.

He wanted Tess to be that woman. The moment she stepped through the doors, he could see it so perfectly in his mind's eye. She belonged here with him—in his house, in his life, in his bed. He'd built this house for her, even though she'd just been a vague longing at the time and not a flesh-and-blood woman.

"It's beautiful," she said, glancing back at him. "It's so open and sunny. And at the same time it's quiet and cool. Serene," she murmured. "That's a good word for it."

Perhaps that's why he was so obsessed with Tess. She rejected him at nearly every turn, but one sweet word, one offhand compliment, and he forgot all the confusion and frustration she'd brought him. "That's what I was going for," Drew said. "I used a lot of natural materials. Stone and wood. I built the staircase myself."

"It's not at all what you usually see in the South. Half the homes in Atlanta look like Tara. But this is different. It's refreshing." She took his arm again and smiled. "Show me the rest."

They strolled through the house, their hands linked. Drew answered her questions, surprised at her keen sense of design and delighted with her appreciation of his talents. For the first time since their evening in the alley, he felt her lower her guard. Though she was reserved, she'd dropped her defenses and spoke to him with honesty and openness. Whatever had caused her shift in attitude, he hoped he could make it last.

They ventured into his bedroom near the end of the tour. He watched as Tess deftly avoided looking at his bed and instead went right to the windows that overlooked the rear of the property. He joined her there, slipping his arms around her waist and pulling her gently back against him.

"That's nice," she said with a sigh.

He nuzzled her neck. "Mmm, it is nice. It feels so good to touch you again."

"I—I meant the view," she said, slipping out of his arms. Tess crossed the room to stand by the bed and stared down at it. As if she was chilled, she rubbed her arms, hugging them close. "Nice bed," she murmured. "Very…big."

"I don't get much chance to sleep in it," Drew said. "Lately I haven't been home a lot. After two months in Tokyo, I'd forgotten what it felt like to get a good night's sleep."

"When were you in Tokyo?"

"I got back the night we met."

She turned around and faced him, a confused frown creasing her pretty features. "Right. You hadn't had anything to eat. I remember."

He slowly approached the bed, watching her wary gaze, wondering what was going through her mind. Her expression had gone blank and she looked at him now with a curious detachment. "I'm glad you decided to come over," he said, reaching out to take her hands.

He bent closer, waiting for some sign, watching for some response. Lord, he wanted to pull her against him and kiss her until she melted in his arms. He could taste her already, those sweet, damp lips that reminded him of summer berries. Her gaze darted to his mouth, then back to his eyes.

And then he couldn't wait any longer. With a deep moan, he drew her to him and covered her mouth with his. All her inhibitions seemed to dissolve. She wrapped her arms around his neck and returned his kiss, her mouth frantic against his, her body pliant beneath his hands.

Slowly, he drew her over to the edge of his bed and pulled her down on top of him. Drew's head spun with sensations that threatened to drive him mad with wanting. Her body pressed against his, her hips shifted until he grew hard with need.

Tiny, urgent sounds escaped her throat and he cupped her face in his palms and plunged deep into the warm recesses of her mouth. She was everything he wanted in a woman, so sweet and alluring, filled with tempting contradictions. One moment distant, and the next, raging with passion. His ears rang and his pulse thrummed in his head. Drew slid his hand along her hip, across her belly, then cupped her breast through her thin silk blouse.

She sighed, covering his fingers with hers. He kneaded her warm flesh, exciting her nipple to a hard bud before moving to the buttons of her blouse. Once again the ringing in his ears intruded, obliterating the sound of her quickened breathing.

Then, suddenly, she pushed away from him and looked down into his eyes. "Bells," she said, blinking away the haze of passion that clouded her pretty green eyes.

"You hear them, too?" Drew asked, pleased. Fireworks and angel choirs had been reputed to accompany passion, but he'd never heard of bells in the midst of a sexual encounter. It was good to know that Tess was affected by their embrace in the same way, though.

She scrambled off him and nervously smoothed her skirt, pushing it down from around her thighs. Color flushed her cheeks and her dark hair tumbled riotously around her face. "I—I think it's the doorbell," she said.

Drew pushed up on his elbow and held out his hand. "It's not the doorbell, Tess." Another soft ring sounded, this time echoing through the house instead of his brain. He flopped back on the bed and groaned, throwing his arm over his eyes. "It is the doorbell."

"Don't you think you should get it? It might be important."

Drew rolled off the bed to his feet. "Stay here. Don't move. I'll be right back."

He left her standing near the bedroom door, her hands clutched in front of her, a nervous smile twitching at her lips. As he descended the stairs, Drew muttered a soft oath. An interruption was the last thing he needed right now. Even if he returned to the bedroom immediately, the moment was ruined. Not because his desire might have cooled—there wasn't a chance in a million of that.

It was ruined because Tess became a different woman every time he turned around.

6

DREW EXPECTED his housekeeper to be waiting on the other side of the door. She had an irritating habit of forgetting her key. Or perhaps it was a messenger from the office with the blueprints for the Gresham Park project. He'd promised to look them over that evening. He pulled open the door. "This better be good."

It wasn't the housekeeper who stood on the other side, or a messenger. Elliot Cosgrove stumbled through the open door, his arms filled with packages and a large blow-up doll tucked under his arm. "I'm sorry, sir, but I thought you'd want to see this."

Drew stepped back and stared, realizing that the doll Elliot carried, with its lush plastic curves and perpetually open mouth, was the type that some men found sexually...comforting. He groaned inwardly. From talking to dogs to sleeping with vinyl companions, Elliot had definitely lost his grip. He'd have to have a serious talk with his business manager. Unfortunately, now was not the time.

Elliot dropped the packages on the polished hardwood floor of the foyer, before he proceeded to wrestle the doll into a Stickley chair. But she refused to sit and kept sliding onto the floor, lying provocatively at Elliot's feet. He finally gave her a good kick and sent her skidding to the base of the stairway.

"Elliot, would you like to introduce your friend?" Drew asked.

"She doesn't belong to me, sir," Elliot replied. "She's yours."

Drew shook his head. "I know I've been having a few problems in the romance department, but I'm sure I don't need—"

"I don't mean she's yours, sir. I mean, she was delivered to your office this afternoon. Along with some other interesting paraphernalia." He dug into an open box. "There's a whip and some handcuffs. And a...a rather large...a large rubber..." Elliot smiled ruefully. "Well, we had to open it. The delivery man insisted on an inventory before we signed for the packages."

Drew winced, then cursed out loud. "I get the picture. And how many clients were in the reception area this time?"

"Just a few," Elliot said. "Mr. Landers from the Sutton Park project and Mr. Cartwright from Denham Plaza."

Drew paced the length of the foyer, his gaze fixed on the boxes and his anger growing. "I want Lubich to pay. I want him out of the picture on the civic center project. I don't care if we have to lower our bid until we're below cost. What he's doing is harassment and I want the civic center committee—hell, I want all Atlanta—to know about his dirty tricks."

"It's not Lubich, sir," Elliot said in a small voice.

Drew turned around and looked at him. "Lubich. His lackeys. What's the difference?"

"Not his lackeys, either."

"Then who?"

"Sir, I think you better sit down while I explain."

Elliot was clearly distraught, though Drew couldn't understand why this latest trick would cause such an emotional reaction. Elliot's hands shook and a sheen of perspiration dotted his forehead. Cosgrove took business way too seriously at times. "Calm down, Elliot, and just tell me what you know. Tess is here and I don't want to keep her waiting."

Elliot gasped. "She's here? You let that woman in your house?" He moaned, then tumbled into the same chair the doll had occupied a few minutes before. His white-knuckled fingers rubbed his forehead and a flush crept from his collar to his round cheeks.

"I think you better explain yourself," Drew said, impatience seeping into his tone. What the hell did Cosgrove have against Tess? If memory served, he'd never set eyes on her.

Elliot buried his face in his hands. "It's her, sir," he said between his fingers. "It's Tess Ryan. *She's* the one who's doing this."

A sharp laugh burst from Drew's throat and dissolved into a chuckle. "Where did you get that harebrained idea? Tess Ryan? Why would she possibly want to embarrass me? I just met her."

"It's me she wants to embarrass. But she thinks you're me. Or I'm you." Elliot drew a long breath and slowly composed himself. "After I tell you this, I'm sure you're going to fire me, so I just want to say, up front, that I've enjoyed working with you, sir. And I think that you're one of the most talented and—"

"Elliot, spit it out!"

His explanation erupted in one long stream, without pause or punctuation. "While you were in Tokyo I pretended to be you to impress a woman and she fell in love with you and your house and your car and then when you came back I had to break up with her before she found out the truth and I think I'm in love with her.'' He paused. ''Sir.''

''You pretended to be *me* to impress a woman?'' Drew considered the confession for a long moment. Though the notion was a bit bizarre, he could understand Elliot's motivation. The trappings of success were attractive to a certain type of woman and Drew had met more than his share of mercenary beauties. ''So you used my car and my house...and my name?''

Elliot nodded, shamefaced. ''And your dog, sir.''

''And it worked?'' Drew asked, an edge of sarcasm coloring his voice.

He blinked in surprise. ''Yes, sir. She fell in love with me. Or—or you. And I fell in love with her. But you can see why I couldn't let it go on. So I put an end to it.''

''And what the hell does this have to do with Tess?''

Elliot swallowed convulsively, his face flushing a deeper shade of red. ''The woman I dumped was her sister, Lucy. We met at that symphony fund-raiser and I was holding your invitation and she just assumed that I was you and then it got out of hand and I couldn't stop myself. She was so beautiful and I'm just so...average. And I didn't realize she was Tess's sister until a few weeks ago. Lucy uses her married name, but she mentioned her sister several times. Tess Ryan. I didn't make the connection until you said her name in the office that day.''

''And you think Tess is the one who—''

''I know it, sir,'' Elliot stated. ''The private investigator you hired discovered that her credit card was used to place this order at the Pleasure Palace. And the stripper finally admitted, for a rather large sum of your money, that a woman hired her. A woman with dark hair and green eyes. I understand Ms. Ryan has green eyes?''

''That could have been her sister.''

"Oh, Lucy isn't the type. I mean, she's not a very organized person. And not at all vindictive. I—I think Tess Ryan is out to get you."

"Because you dumped her sister?"

"No, sir. She thinks *you* dumped her sister."

"But I don't even know her sister!"

"I realize that, sir, and I'm very sorry about that. But you wouldn't be attracted to her if you did know her. Lucy's not really your type and she's—"

"Damn it, Elliot, stop talking for a minute so I can figure this all out!" Drew sat down on the bottom step and stared at the naked doll. Her empty gaze seemed to mock his confusion. What the hell was going on? Was he really supposed to believe that Tess Ryan was up to no good? That she had let the air out of his tires and hired the stripper?

Everything he had shared with her had been turned upside down. Had she deliberately shoved that tray of crab claws into his hands at the reception? Was she purposefully trying to play hard to get as part of some grand scheme to drive him crazy? And what had she really been doing at his gate this afternoon when he drove up?

"Sir?" Elliot interrupted in a meek voice. "Should I clean out my desk now or tomorrow morning?"

Drew pushed off the step and stood. "You're not fired, Cosgrove. We all do some pretty stupid things for love. Besides, I may need your help."

Elliot stood, indignation suffusing his features. "I'm here for you, sir," he said. "We'll confront her right this minute and then we'll toss her out of your house."

Clutching Elliot's shoulder, Drew pushed him back down in the chair. "No. I don't want you to reveal any of this to anyone. I want your word on that. As far as we're concerned, we still suspect Lubich."

"But shouldn't you—"

"If Tess is out for some petty little revenge, I'll find out soon enough. But until then, I think I'll get a little revenge of my own."

Drew's gaze followed the rise of the stairs and he wondered what Tess was doing this very moment in his bedroom. If Elliot was telling the truth, she was probably rifling through his belongings or short-sheeting his bed. Tess had been deceiving him. At the least, she'd neglected to mention her sister. But worse, she might be planning another little trick to drive him crazy.

But he had a little plan of his own. He would bide his time, he'd keep an eye on her and he'd wait for her to slip up. And whether that came before or after she admitted she loved him didn't really make a difference. She couldn't deny what was in her heart for much longer.

TESS STOOD in the center of Drew's bedroom, staring at his bed. She pinched her eyes shut and tried to imagine Lucy lying beneath the sheets, hoping the image would provide a just punishment for her betrayal. She had kissed Drew Wyatt again. Only this time, it was much worse. This time, she'd lost control, she'd enjoyed his touch. And she had wanted more.

From the moment he took her into his arms and tumbled her onto the bed, she had forgotten her sister and thought only of herself, of her needs and desires. "I'm a horrible sister," she murmured. If the doorbell hadn't rung, who knows how far she would have gone?

But what was she to do? It was just bad luck that Lucy had met Andrew Wyatt first. If Drew had dumped anyone else, Tess wouldn't think twice about falling in love with him. Did that make her a bad person? Was it wrong to think of Lucy as just another faceless, nameless woman from his not-too-distant past?

"I'm the stuff that bad talk shows are made of. She's In Love With Her Sister's Man!" With a soft oath, she turned away from the bed and walked to the bedroom door. Maybe she could sneak out without having to talk to Drew again. And perhaps, if he never saw her again, he might forget the intimacies they had shared.

Fat chance! Drew seemed bound and determined to cultivate an intimate relationship. She'd rejected him at nearly every turn and he'd kept coming back for more. Either he was a card-carrying masochist or he truly harbored strong feelings for her. Tess wanted to believe the latter, that Lucy was just a little bump in the road, a pothole perhaps, on the way to Drew's true romantic destiny.

So what were Tess's choices? She could walk out of his house, knowing full well that he'd come after her. She could throw caution to the wind and follow her passions, keeping everything a secret from Lucy. Or she could tell both Drew and Lucy the truth and let the Hummels fall where they may.

Slipping out the front door unnoticed seemed like the best option for now. Tess glanced in the mirror over his dresser, straightened her blouse and drew a long breath. For good measure, she slipped off her shoes before she started for the stairs.

The foyer was silent as she reached the top of the staircase. Wincing, she took the first step down, then another. When she reached the landing, she caught sight of the front door and her heart fell. Drew stood, his back against that very door, his gaze fixed on a mess of boxes scattered on the floor.

"Who was at the door?" she asked in a quiet voice.

He looked up at her with a startled expression, as if

he'd forgotten she was in the house. Then he stepped forward and gathered the boxes in his arms. "Are you hungry? I'll make you some dinner." At the last minute, he grabbed an oddly shaped balloon, then disappeared into the rear of the house.

To her relief, he didn't expect them to return to the bedroom, though she couldn't ignore the sliver of regret she felt. She'd never know what might have happened between them. But maybe that was for the best. Reluctantly, she followed in his direction, taking one last look at the front door before she headed to the kitchen. Certainly she could exert some measure of self-control in the kitchen.

Like the rest of the house, the kitchen was an amazing combination of form and function. Sleek wooden cabinets and shiny marble countertops glowed softly under the natural light streaming through floor-to-ceiling windows. Compared to the kitchen at her house, it was painfully tidy and efficient.

Like the bedroom upstairs, the kitchen and adjacent great room overlooked the backyard, with one wall made up entirely of windows. Drew stood at one of those windows now, his attention fixed on the sunny outdoors, his mood oddly distant.

"Sit down," he said distractedly, motioning to the trio of stools that lined the breakfast bar. "Would you like something to drink? A glass of wine?"

Nodding, she slid onto a stool, then noticed the balloon on the stool at the end of the marble counter. On second glance, she realized it wasn't a balloon at all, but a giant doll. A giant, naked doll. Bewildered, she looked over at Drew who had moved to the refrigerator. When he straightened, holding a bottle of wine, he made no move to explain the third member of their dinner party. In truth, he acted as if they were still…alone.

Finally, Tess could stand it no longer. "Who's the other woman?" she asked. "Old girlfriend?" Her lips quirked at the little joke, but her clever comment drew no reaction from him.

He placed a wineglass in front of her and filled it with a pale yellow Chardonnay. "A gift. She was delivered to my office late this afternoon, along with some other interesting items." He shoved a small box in her direction. "Open it."

Tess stared at the box and silently cursed her sister. This had Lucy written all over it. She reached into the box and withdrew a pair of bikini underpants made of a strange, sticky fabric.

"Edible," Drew said in a sarcastic tone. "I thought we'd save them for dessert. I have a bottle of port that would complement them nicely."

A giggle slipped from Tess's lips and she tossed the underwear back in the box. "I don't think I'll have room for dessert tonight." She picked up her wineglass. "You seem to be taking this rather well," she ventured.

"Do I?" He paused, meeting her eyes, his eyebrow arched. "Looks can be deceiving."

Tess squirmed on the stool, uncomfortable with the hard set of his jaw, the cool angle of his gaze. "What are you going to do?"

He braced his elbows on the counter and leaned toward her. "I was hoping you could help."

"Me? How could I—"

"You're a creative person, Tess. Maybe you could help me plan a little payback?"

"I'm not sure I understand."

"You know. Revenge. A way to get back at Lubich for

all the trouble he's caused me. I've lost valuable business because of him. And I want to even the score.''

The icy look in his eyes frightened her. She'd never believed that Drew had a cold and calculating side, but it was showing now. "I—I'm really not the person you should ask about—"

"Oh, but you are! After all, you have experience with this kind of thing.''

Tess gulped convulsively and carefully set her glass down. He knew! Somehow he had found out that she and Lucy were behind all these tricks and now he was going to punish her for it. But first, he was going to play around with her, like a cat with a cornered mouse. "Wha—what do you mean?''

"You're a woman," he said. "Women are so much better at these little acts of vengeance and deceit than men. I just assumed you could give me some advice.''

Tess wasn't sure whether to be insulted or relieved. How dare he say such a thing! She was neither underhanded nor deceitful—as long as you didn't count her behavior of the past week, for which she had a perfectly sound excuse. She wasn't really the one perpetrating the petty crimes of revenge, she was only the catalyst. The unwitting, remorseful busybody that set this whole mess in motion. "I don't think I'd be good at that," she murmured. "Besides, aren't there better ways to stop this...problem?''

"What would you suggest? The police? Or maybe the FBI? I suppose I could file a lawsuit.''

"No!" Tess cried. "I—I would take a more lenient approach. Maybe you should talk to the man. Get his side of the story and then ask him—politely—to stop.''

Drew pushed back from the counter. "I'm really more

of an action kind of guy. Talking is for wimps. I suppose I could confront Lubich…his nose with my fist.''

Tess gasped. ''You'd resort to physical violence?''

Drew considered her question for a long moment, then shrugged and smiled, his edgy mood lifting in the blink of an eye. ''Nah. I'll just have to think of something that hurts more. So what do you want for dinner? We can have hot dogs, grilled cheese or frozen pizza.''

''I really think we should talk about this need for retaliation,'' Tess insisted. ''It's not healthy.'' This was poetic justice, Tess lecturing *him* about the evils of revenge. She had never condoned Lucy's actions—it had all started as an exercise in simple closure. But she did have the capacity to stop her sister—and Drew. All she had to do was admit the truth.

''And *I* think we should talk about us instead. I'm glad you decided to stop by, Tess.'' He reached across the counter and took her hand, then drew it to his mouth. His lips brushed the inside of her wrist, leaving a warm brand on her skin. Tess closed her eyes and savored the sweet sensations that shot through her bloodstream.

''Cheese,'' Tess said on a sigh, imagining his lips in other delicious, mind-numbing spots. Below her ear, on her shoulder, along the curve of her breast.

He'd moved up to the soft skin in the hollow of her elbow. ''Cheese?''

She cleared her throat and swallowed hard. ''I think I'd like a toasted cheese sandwich for dinner.'' Dinner would be good right now. Cooking dinner would be even better. For if Drew didn't make her a toasted cheese sandwich right this instant, Tess was certain she was about to become the main course in Drew's private little feast.

STARS GLITTERED in a black velvet sky as Tess and Drew strolled down the brick driveway. Rufus tagged along at

their heels, running off every now and then to chase some
imaginary prey. It was nearly 9:00 p.m. and the moon
hung low on the horizon, bathing the landscape in a soft,
hazy light. A mockingbird called from the top of a tall
cedar, its song sweet and plaintive.

"It's a beautiful night," Tess said softly. She stifled a
yawn, then sighed. Exhaustion dogged her steps and she
leaned into his body. Drew slipped his arm around her
waist and pulled her close, kissing the top of her head.

This was the way it was supposed to be between them,
Tess mused. Easy and comfortable. After their rather tense
conversation about revenge, Drew's mood had relaxed
considerably. He had joked and teased and charmed her
until she completely forgot all her worries and misgivings
about Lucy and Lubich.

They had shared a simple dinner of sandwiches and
soup, and then retired to his terrace with a bottle of wine
and idle conversation. They spoke of the past, of childhood dreams and teenage loves. They talked of careers
and hopes for the future. And for long stretches of time,
she forgot about Lucy, about all the lies she'd been forced
to tell, all the guilt she'd buried for so long.

She'd been given one night to see the potential of what
she shared with Drew Wyatt. And it took her only one
moment to realize that she never wanted to let him go.
She had a right to be happy, didn't she? Lucy never
seemed to let anything stand in the way of what *she*
wanted, so why should Tess? And had their roles been
reversed, Tess had serious doubts that Lucy would reject
a man simply because he'd dated her sister. In fact, Lucy
used to steal her boyfriends all the time!

So Tess would take her happiness where she found it
and she'd enjoy it as long as it lasted. And if it lasted a

week or a lifetime, she wouldn't allow herself to feel ashamed.

When they reached the gate, Drew unlocked it and pulled it open for her. She stepped through, then turned to face him. Her eyes skimmed his features, trying to memorize them in the soft moonlight, knowing she'd see him again in her dreams. "Thank you for dinner," she said.

Drew leaned forward and brushed his lips against hers. The kiss was soft and fleeting and so tantalizing. "I don't want you to leave," he murmured against her mouth.

Tess felt a warm blush crawl up her cheeks. "I don't want to leave."

"Then don't," he said. "Stay. Spend the night."

Her breath caught and she looked up at him, surprised at his bold request, and severely tempted to acquiesce. What was he suggesting? Did he simply want to continue their conversation on the terrace? Or was he asking for more? Tess suspected that he didn't have conversation in mind. Not by the dark desire in his eyes.

She drew a shaky breath and fought the impulse to turn around and follow him into the house…into his bedroom and into the pleasures of passion. It was too soon. She wasn't ready for this. Making love with Drew Wyatt was a step she wasn't ready to take, not with so many lies standing between them.

Still, what would guarantee that she'd ever get the chance again? Tess knew it would be wonderful to surrender to his touch. Drew was a passionate man, a man who could make her blood warm and her heart sing with just a simple caress, a careless kiss. She imagined the two of them together, caught in a naked embrace, limbs tangled and nothing between them but skin.

"I—I can't stay," she said, her voice tight in her throat. "I have work tomorrow."

His hand skimmed her cheek, then drifted lower to brush against her breast. A tingle began at his touch, spreading through her body, weakening her resolve. Tess tried to focus on Lucy, but no matter how hard she tried, she couldn't bring her sister to mind.

His hands moved over her body and his lips explored her face, gently stealing every rational thought from her head until she forgot who he was, who *she* was. Yes, this was right. This was good. This was so—

"Wrong!" Tess cried.

Drew's hands froze and he slowly opened his eyes to gaze down at her.

"I—I'm sorry," she said, shaking her head. "I just can't. I'm not ready for this. I mean, I'm ready, in one sense. I'm *really* ready. But I'm just not..."

"Ready?" Drew asked, his eyebrow quirking up.

Tess smiled and pressed her forehead against his chest. "I better go."

"Then go," he said. "Go, before I pick you up and carry you back inside with me."

Tess pushed up on her toes and kissed his cheek, then turned and ran across the street. When she finally reached her car, she glanced back at Drew. He stood watching her, Rufus sitting obediently at his feet, tail swishing across the brick driveway.

"Say good-night, Rufus," Drew called.

The dog woofed once, then laid down with his chin on his front paws.

She gave them both a wave, then climbed into her car and pulled out onto the street. But as she drove away, the impact of what had passed between them hit her like a ten-ton truck. Her heart began to race and she found herself struggling to breathe.

Finally, Tess yanked the wheel to the right and the car bumped up against the curb. "Oh, dear," she murmured, pressing her palm to her chest. "Oh my, oh my. What could you have been thinking?"

She wasn't thinking, that was the problem! She was lusting and panting and quivering. Well, it wouldn't happen again. Not until this little game of revenge was over and done with. Not until he knew that the woman he'd spurned just a few short weeks ago was her sister, Lucy. And not until poor Mr. Lubich was vindicated for crimes that he hadn't committed.

Then—and only then—would she be ready.

7

THE TRAFFIC in downtown Atlanta was thick with the evening rush. Tess squinted against the sun as she tried to catch the address of a passing building. Drew had called her office earlier that afternoon and left a message to meet him for dinner at six. He left no explanation, just an address and a sense of urgency.

Tess rubbed her eyes and yawned as she waited for a stoplight to turn green. As soon as she'd straightened out this mess she had managed to make, she was going to take a nice, long nap. After Drew's vow of retaliation against his business rival, poor Mr. Lubich, Tess had no choice but to keep an eye on him. She didn't want *him* to do anything that *she* might regret later. So they'd spent the last three evenings together. Thankfully, he'd made no further mention of his plans for revenge—or his need to have her in his bed.

He had, however, done his best to charm her and pamper her and convince her that they were made for each other. Wonderful restaurants, a symphony concert, a jazz club, a romantic movie. Late nights spent sipping coffee at a local coffeehouse followed by long, lazy kisses and even longer goodbyes before she drove home.

They usually met after work at his downtown office and said goodbye at her car, but Tess knew that would soon change. How long would it be before Drew began to wonder about where she lived, or who she lived with? How long before he pressed her for details about her personal life? Tess wasn't sure, but she did know that when that day came, she'd be forced to tell him the truth. Until then, she just wanted to enjoy the time they spent together.

Still, Tess wasn't sure how long *she* could go on under the cloud of her charade. During the day, in between her duties at work, she worried about what Lucy was up to. She'd nearly convinced her sister that if she hadn't achieved closure yet, that door might just swing back in the other direction and hit her squarely in the face. Lucy reacted well to the metaphor since it involved her face rather than the lukewarm threat of arrest. But Tess wasn't quite sure that Lucy was ready to give up on her tricks.

During the evenings, when Tess spent time with Drew, she tried to avert any disaster he might initiate and tried to think of something other than kissing him. The threat of his private investigator niggled at her mind, an always present worry that Drew might find out the truth before Tess worked up the courage to tell him.

And then, late at night, she would lie awake in bed, wondering when the next shoe would drop. "It's like living in a shoe store in the middle of an earthquake," Tess muttered, still squinting at building numbers. "Sooner or later, there will be a thud." She just wasn't sure where it would come from, or from whom.

Tess glanced down at the address scribbled on the message slip. She'd circled the block twice and couldn't find the building. Every address on the north side of the street had an odd number and she had an even. And the only thing on the south side of the street was a construction site. She pulled her car into a parking spot and leaned over to read the huge sign in front of the site.

"Denham Plaza," she read. "Wyatt and Associates, Architects." This must be the place. But how was she supposed to find Drew on such a large site? Men and machinery cluttered the area around the building's steel skeleton. Tess stepped out of the car and headed toward a gate in the chain-link fence. A small trailer designated Office sat just beyond the gate.

She walked in that direction but then stopped short when she saw a group a disreputable-looking men loitering near the fence. They watched her from beneath the brims of their hard hats, their beefy arms crossed over flannel-clad chests. Tess shook her head, knowing what was coming. Either they'd whistle and hoot, embarrassing her to the core. Or they'd barely notice her as she passed, shredding her ego in the process. She wasn't sure which would be worse.

But as she stepped through the gate, the largest member of the group moved toward her. She froze and glanced over her shoulder, wondering if she could outrun the guy. He was built more like a rhino than a gazelle and she was pretty sure she could take him in a footrace, even in high heels and a tight skirt.

"Miss Ryan?"

Tess blinked. How did this man know her name? "Yes," she said in a hesitant voice. "I'm Tess Ryan."

His face split into a boyish ear-to-ear grin which did much to dispel his tough-guy image. "I'm Ed, the construction foreman here. Mr. Wyatt says we're supposed to bring you upstairs to where he is."

Tess stared at the group of five men. "All of you?"

Ed nodded. "Me and the boys are gonna make sure you don't get yourself hurt." He produced a hard hat from behind his back. Tess's name had been artfully inscribed on the front. "You're to put this on, miss, and we'll take you right up."

Tess glanced back once more, then forced a smile as

she placed the hat on her head. Ed looked as if he could bench-press a Buick, not the kind of man who took no for an answer. She quickly convinced herself that there was no reason to worry about her safety around these men, especially if Drew trusted them. Reluctantly, she nodded. "Let's go."

Ed frowned, then cleared his throat. "Ah, we can't go up just yet, Miss Ryan." He glared at the man with Rudy emblazoned on his hard hat.

Rudy stared back mutely. Realization slowly dawned and with a nervous flourish, he swept a huge bouquet of flowers from behind his back. He stepped up to her and offered her the roses. "These are for you," he said. "I—I almost forgot. Sorry, miss."

Tess smiled. "Thank you, Rudy. They're beautiful."

A blush flooded his ruddy cheeks. "Them flowers ain't from me. They'd be from Mr. Wyatt."

"I know. But they're beautiful nonetheless," she murmured as she followed Ed to the entrance. The five other men surrounded her, two on each side and one directly behind her. They escorted her through a tangle of building materials to a huge cage. Ed opened the door and motioned her inside.

She hesitated and Rudy leaned over. "It's the elevator, miss. I know it looks a little scary, but you're perfectly safe with us."

Tess drew a calming breath then stepped to the rear of the elevator cage. The five men followed and she wondered how the elevator would get off the ground with their combined weight. But then the cage jerked upward at an amazing rate of speed and she gulped, her ears popping. Up and up they rose, skimming along the outside of the building until the city lay spread out behind and below them. Numbers flashed by on the girders outside, first twenties, then thirties. Tess started to panic when they reached the forties. The elevator stopped at fifty-five and Ed opened the door.

She could see the sky through the steel skeleton, feel the cool breeze buffeting her body. Tess nearly asked Ed to take her back down again, not sure she could handle the height. But the construction foreman held out his hand and led her along a trail of gridded walkways. Finally, to Tess's relief, they found a spot that had a real floor.

Laid out on the floor was a checkered blanket and all the makings of a picnic. Standing nearby, his shoulder braced on a girder, Drew watched her approach. He was dressed like the others, in a faded flannel shirt, limb-hugging jeans and a hard hat. "Thanks, Ed," he called, pushing away from the girder. "I'll keep an eye on her now."

Ed and his gang disappeared back into the elevator, leaving the two of them alone at the top of the city. "Did you have trouble finding the place?" Drew asked, holding out his hand. He led her to the blanket that he'd placed near the outside edge of the building, a little too near for Tess's comfort. But she pushed aside her fears and sat down.

"We're having dinner up here?"

"Best sunsets in Atlanta," he said. "And when the skies get dark, you can see the stars and the city lights and the planes landing at the airport."

"I'm not real fond of heights," Tess said. "I almost fell out of the booth at the Tiki Palace if you remember. There's no telling what might happen here."

"I'll keep you safe," he replied, sitting down beside her. "Besides, I chose this place on purpose. I didn't want you running off at the first sign of a serious conversation." He met her gaze squarely, unflinchingly. "Because that's what we're going to have here tonight, Tess. A serious conversation."

Tess's breath froze in her throat and a knot of nerves twisted in her stomach. He knew! His private detective had hit pay dirt and now Drew knew the whole story. She reached out and grabbed the glass of wine that he had poured for her and took a gulp.

Would he just break it off quickly and cleanly? Or would he demand answers and apologies? Tess glanced back toward the elevator. Oh, what a cruel man, to trap her up here with no chance for escape. He probably meant to torture her with his accusations, exact retribution for her deceptions. "I—I know exactly why you brought me here," Tess began.

Drew frowned. "You do?"

"So go ahead. Get it over with. I'm not afraid to hear what you have to say. In fact, I welcome it. I've been waiting for this to happen and I—"

"Are you just about through?" Drew asked. "Because if you are, then maybe I can get a word in here."

Chastened, Tess pressed her lips together and dropped her gaze to her wineglass. "Go ahead."

"I don't know what you think I'm planning to say, but I brought you here to talk about our future."

With a gasp, Tess looked up at him. "Future?"

"Yes. Our future. The next month, the next year. Maybe the rest of our lives if everything goes well."

Tess's heart swelled and emotion clogged her throat until she could barely breathe. "You—you think we have a future?"

"Isn't it obvious, Tess? I can hardly think about anything else."

Tess paused. How could they possibly have a future with so much standing between them? Everything they shared had been built on a foundation of lies. And if those lies were revealed, their entire relationship might collapse beneath them. "Things are moving so fast."

"Exactly. And that's why I think we need to get to know each other better. I need to meet your friends and your family. See where you live. And I think you should meet my parents. They'll be in town next month and I'm sure they'd love to get to know you."

"Your parents?" Tess winced inwardly, pushing back a rising wave of alarm. This was not what she expected. It would have been better that he'd learned the truth, that he'd ranted and raved and then ordered her out of his life. She could have handled that.

Drew sighed and pulled off his hard hat, tossing it on the blanket in front of them. He raked his hand through his hair. "Am I wrong, Tess? I thought things were going well between us. These past few days have been wonderful. We've grown closer, we've shared so much. And you can't deny the physical attraction."

Why couldn't this have waited? All she needed was a few more days to work up her courage. But now, she was faced with a choice—a choice between Drew's love and Lucy's wrath. A choice between lust and loyalty. "Yes," she agreed. "We are attracted to each other."

"So what's the holdup, Tess? Is it me? Is there another man? Why can't you acknowledge that we might just have a future together?"

"I can!" she snapped, slamming her wineglass down. She closed her eyes and calmed her shaken nerves. "I— I can," she repeated in an even voice. "But everything is so complicated and I don't have a lot of experience in this kind of thing."

"Tess, this isn't rocket science. Or quantum physics. You go with your heart. How do you feel?"

"I feel good," Tess offered, knowing how feeble her words sounded. Good. Such a generic word and such an understatement for how he made her heart sing and her senses spin. But he was asking for more than she was ready to offer. She wasn't ready to tell him the truth. Not yet. It was too soon.

But, if he insisted on this new phase in their relationship, she'd be forced to reveal everything. He'd come over to her house and he'd... Tess paused. She'd never realized it before, but Drew had probably been to her house. In fact, he might already know about her family through Lucy. Though Lucy did spend the majority of her time talking about herself, she had to have mentioned her sister. Maybe not by name, but...

Suddenly, her mind became tangled with confusion. He and Lucy had been together for two months. There must have been at least one mention of Tess's name. He'd never made the connection between Tess Ryan and Lucy Ryan, but that was obviously because Lucy preferred to go by one of her married names, Courault or Battenfield or Oleska. But, somewhere in their conversations, she should have dropped at least one—

"Tess?"

She jumped, startled by his voice. "What?"

"You looked like you were a million miles away. Are you all right?"

"I'm just...hungry," she said, folding her hands on her lap. "Maybe we should eat."

"Then you'll think about what I said?" he asked, leaning closer and taking her hand. He laced his fingers with hers and softly stroked the back of her hand with his thumb, a movement so familiar and so distracting.

"Yes," she murmured. Tess took another long sip of wine. "I will think about it. I promise."

Tess watched as he laid out their picnic dinner. Oh, she'd think about it, all right. That's all she'd be able to do for the next twenty-four hours. And she'd finally come to a conclusion. It was time to tell him the truth.

And time to put an end to a relationship that had never really begun.

THE ELEVATOR DROPPED floor by floor, the metal cage clattering in the silent night air. Drew felt Tess's hand tighten around his and he gave her fingers a squeeze. "It's perfectly safe," he said, glancing over at her.

His gaze traced her beautiful features, outlined by the harsh light from the overhead bulb. He'd dreamed of that face every night since they'd met, fantasized about her slender body. How had Tess Ryan managed to capture his heart and soul with so little effort? An objective observer might conclude that she barely cared for him. But Drew had to believe there were deeper feelings lingering just below the surface, feelings that she was compelled to hide for the moment.

He wanted—no, needed—to know what those feelings were. So he'd decided to give her a little push. Drew knew he had forced the issue with his talk of the future. But if she couldn't admit to her little acts of revenge, she might choose to put him out of her life altogether. He'd also placed himself in a tricky spot. After all, he could have gone to her as soon as Elliot told him the whole silly story. But he'd chosen to keep it quiet, to test the truth of her feelings for him, to give her a chance to come clean and confess.

Maybe he'd made a mistake, drawing this out so long, carefully steering her toward a confession of her actions and her feelings. But he still couldn't trust Tess. Every sweet word, every alluring smile, could all be an act. She could be leading him on, drawing him in, then setting him up for the final blow. Could Tess be that devious?

Drew slowly released his tightly held breath. If she was, he didn't plan to give her the satisfaction of besting him in this little game they were playing. If it all fell apart, he'd be sure to come out of it with his heart intact and his pride in one piece. Or would he?

The thought of Tess anywhere but in his life brought on a flood of anxiety. Why couldn't *she* have told him the minute *she* knew? The same instant he revealed who he was? Unless their first meeting had been set up from the start and she'd never intended to tell him.

He had a hard time believing she was capable of such a coldhearted scheme. In truth, he'd been having a hard time remembering there was any scheme at all! When they were together, all his doubts seemed to fade and he was left only with those incredible green eyes, eyes that spoke volumes more that Tess could ever say out loud.

Maybe there was no scheme anymore. There hadn't been a single dirty trick in nearly a week. Could he risk believing that her feelings for him had overwhelmed her quest for vengeance? That she wanted the past to fade into the past as much as he did? If she could forgive and forget, so could he.

The elevator came to an abrupt stop and Drew looked out to find the cage on the ground level. He reached out and opened the door, then took Tess's arm and led her through the dimly lit yard. When they reached the street, he slipped his arm around her shoulders. "So, you'll think about what I said?"

"Yes," she said.

Drew's jaw tightened at the distant tone of her voice. Why couldn't she just tell him? She had to know he cared. He'd spent the past two weeks showing her and telling her, proving it at every turn. A slow burn of frustration clouded his mind. "I forgot to mention," he began, his words measured, his conscience railing against what he was about to say. He knew he shouldn't, but he couldn't help it. He had to give her one more little push. "Our friend, Lubich? I came up with a perfect little payback."

She froze in her steps a few yards from her car, then slowly turned to him. "You—you did?"

"Day after tomorrow, his house is scheduled to be photographed for the next issue of *Architectural Digest*. Sometime after midnight tomorrow night, five hundred pink plastic flamingos will be planted on his front lawn. The guys from *Architectural Digest* are going to arrive at 227 Compton Court to find it turned into a shrine to tackiness. I think that will send a pointed message, don't you?"

She stared at him for a long moment, then nodded her head. "I'd better be going."

With that, she walked to her car and got inside. She didn't bother to wave goodbye, didn't even look back. As the taillights disappeared into the night, Drew cursed and kicked at the pavement.

If this didn't work, he wasn't sure what would. As far as he could see, this was his last chance. Now all he had to do was find five hundred pink flamingos and arrange to have them put in the front yard of his lawyer's house. Then he'd need to pray that Tess had made careful note of the address and didn't look it up in the phone book for confirmation.

Kip Carpenter wouldn't be too happy about the prospect of the plastic birds, but his attorney was an old college friend and the reason Drew first settled in the Atlanta area. Besides, Drew could almost guarantee that the flamingos would take flight shortly after they landed, thanks to Tess's noble efforts.

"This better work, Tess," he murmured. "Because if it doesn't, I've got no more tricks in my bag."

"SO MANY FLAMINGOS, so little time," Tess muttered as she threw another one of the pink plastic creatures into the rear of the rental truck. It landed on the pile with a thud and she turned back to her task.

To her relief, she had found Mr. Lubich's house shortly after 1:00 a.m. It wasn't hard to spot as it was the only house on Compton Court with lawn ornaments that glowed in the dark. Tess had to admit that Drew's little prank possessed a certain absurd sensibility. The striking home loomed in the darkness, a picture of sophisticated design and artistic pretension. It was meant to convey the image of great wealth, yet that image suffered sorely under the onslaught of five hundred pink flamingos.

She had hoped she might intercept the people who had been hired to plant the birds and was ready to pay them handsomely if they agreed to forget their purpose. But she'd been stuck at a reception she'd planned for a local television station until far past midnight. As it was, she left the caterers to finish the cleanup.

If her luck held, she'd be able to pile the rest of the flamingos inside before the sun came up. And then she would drive them to Drew's house, let herself in the front gate and confess all her sins. She'd made her decision not that instant, but a few minutes after she'd left him at the construction sight the previous night, determined to tell him the truth the very next day.

But when she called his office that morning, he'd been out at a meeting. Wavering between paralyzing doubt and stubborn determination, she'd managed to change her mind at least a hundred times during the day, weighing the pros and cons of each side until she was ready to scream in frustration.

Lucy or Drew. Drew or Lucy. No matter which way she went, she'd risk alienating at least one of them. She'd rented the truck as insurance to cover her indecision, but it only gave her an excuse to chicken out in the end. Now here she was, tossing flamingos into the back of a truck and cursing her cowardice with every breath. But this was the end of it, Tess vowed. When the last flamingo fell, she knew what she had to do.

It took Tess nearly two hours and countless trips back and forth to the truck to clear Lubich's lawn. She had to dive into the bushes twice when she heard passing cars, but neither one turned off the main road into Compton Court and she'd been able to complete the job without being detected.

When at last she shut the door on the flamingos, she was ready to drive home and go to bed. But she knew she had one more task to accomplish before she could close her eyes. As she drove to Drew's house, she went over her speech in her head.

She'd begin with a heartfelt apology and then assure him of the depth of her feelings for him. Then she'd present a brief overview of Lucy's disastrous love life, placing their relationship in the context of Lucy's other men. She'd explain her need to help her sister deal with her problems. After that, she'd berate the work of every psychologist and psychiatrist she'd ever read and tell him how she'd tried to stop Lucy from wreaking havoc on his life.

Finally, if she'd chosen her words carefully and explained her actions in just the right way, he would smile. Maybe he'd even laugh. He would pull her into his arms and forgive her with a long, deep kiss that would last for the rest of the night.

Her thoughts were so occupied with her confession that Tess didn't realize she was close to Drew's house until she pulled up to his front gate. Apprehensively, she sat in the truck for nearly a half hour, replaying her intended confession over and over until she was certain it would elicit the right response.

With a resigned sigh, Tess hopped out of the truck and punched in the gate code. "This is it," she said. "There's no going back now."

The house was dark as she walked up to the front door. Tess drew in a deep breath, then leaned on the doorbell and closed her eyes. It would all be over in a few minutes.

A few seconds later, the lights went on in the foyer and the door swung open. Drew stood in the doorway, a dark silhouette wearing only a pair of boxer shorts and an expression of surprise.

Tess's heart stopped as she took in the sight of him, nearly naked. A soft light gleamed off his smooth skin, shifting over his body with the subtle movements of his muscles. He rubbed his eyes. "Tess? What are you doing here?"

"We need to talk," she said, dragging her gaze from his wide chest and brushing past him into the house. Now was not the time to lust after his body. She was having enough trouble focusing her thoughts and maintaining her resolve. Any contemplation of his body would set her seriously off track.

"It's nearly four in the morning," Drew said, padding after her in his bare feet. "Couldn't this have waited a few more hours?"

Tess strode through the house, back to the kitchen and into the adjacent great room with its soft couches and dim lighting. This would have to be the place, she decided. She flopped down on one of the sofas, threw her arm over her eyes and waited for him to join her. A few seconds later, he was beside her. She could feel the warmth radiating from his bare skin, could smell the last traces of his cologne.

Tess clenched her hands to still the temptation, the almost irresistible need to touch him. She wanted to curl into his arms and press her face into the soft dusting of hair on his chest. It would be so easy to lose herself in his body, surrender to his touch, to replace her resolve with the passion they both held so tightly in check.

He reached out to pull her hand away from her eyes, but Tess stiffened. "Don't," she warned. "I can't look at you when I tell you this."

"All right." He drew his fingers along her arm, then refrained from touching her further. "I'm listening."

His soft voice sent a shiver down her spine. Suddenly, she felt utterly exhausted, as if she couldn't be bothered to think. She barely had the energy to speak, the words that she wanted to say becoming a blurry jumble in her mind.

If he tried to touch her again, she wouldn't resist. She'd toss aside all her noble intentions and she'd lose herself in the feel of him, the scent and taste of him. The thought of making love to Drew Wyatt filled her mind with an overwhelming need. If she turned and looked at him, she'd be lost.

Tess cursed silently, pinching her eyes shut. And if she could just gather her thoughts…just breathe deeply and concentrate…let herself drift…everything would be… all…right…

"Tess?"

"Give me a moment," she murmured, principles and

passion waging a battle for her soul. Breathing deeply, Tess waited for the words to come, but they never did. Seconds passed, then minutes. She became aware of him sitting beside her, of the moment he took her into his arms and pulled her against his body. She even remembered the gentle way he kissed her face, then her mouth. And the way he stroked her body, his hands warm through her clothing, his touch lulling her into a sweet sense of security.

The only thing she didn't remember was falling asleep.

8

TESS SLOWLY OPENED her eyes to bright sunshine streaming through the windows. For a long moment, she lay motionless, enjoying the sense of total relaxation that filled her limbs and fogged her mind. She hadn't slept through the night since before she met Drew. How wonderful that her mind was clear and her mood was—

Drew! With a soft cry, she bolted upright in bed, memories from the previous evening flooding her mind. Scrubbing at her bleary eyes, she squinted at her surroundings. "Oh, no." Tess sighed. She wasn't in *her* bedroom, with her pretty four-poster and her lilac wallpaper and her lace curtains. Somehow, Tess had ended up in *his* bedroom, in his bed—alone, at least for now.

She rewound the memories of the last twelve hours and the events came back to her, first slowly and then in a mortifying rush. The flamingos and the truck. Her confession. Tess racked her brain to remember exactly what she'd told him and how he'd reacted. But nothing came back.

She buried her face in her hands and groaned. There had been no confession. All that determination, all her good intentions gone to waste. To make things worse, she'd—oh, good grief, she'd slept with him! But even more horrible than that, she didn't remember it!

Though she had been exhausted, Tess couldn't believe she'd completely forgotten such a momentous and highly anticipated event. Damn, she wasn't even sure if the encounter had been the biggest mistake she'd ever made—or the most wonderful, passionate experience of her life. She racked her brain once more for some shred of memory, some clue as to what had transpired in Drew Wyatt's bed. With a wince, Tess plucked at the sheets and lifted them up, wondering whether Drew had undressed her slowly and seductively, or whether he had ripped the clothes off her body in a fit of raging passion.

But to her utter surprise, she was partially dressed, still wearing her silk camisole and tap pants. "My panty hose," she murmured. "Oh, thank God for panty hose." She might as well have been wearing a medieval chastity belt, for Tess knew making love while wearing panty hose was virtually impossible. Her honor was still intact, at least as far as Drew was concerned.

Still, mixed with overpowering relief, Tess felt a bit insulted. Was she that easy to resist? He'd obviously put her to bed, but he hadn't been tempted any further. But then, maybe making love to a semiconscious woman wasn't exactly a turn-on for Drew. She pushed back the covers and slipped out of bed.

Tess wasn't about to give him another chance at seduction. A careful search of the room turned up her suit, neatly hung from his closet door, and her shoes, placed beneath it on the floor. She dressed hastily, afraid that Drew might return at any second and catch her in her underwear. It would be much easier to resist him if she were fully dressed.

Strangely, her resolve hadn't diminished since the previous night. In truth, Tess was more determined than ever to tell Drew everything. A good night's sleep had brightened her attitude considerably and she was almost certain she could get through this without an emotional scene.

Tess combed her hair with her fingers, straightened her jacket and headed downstairs. Drew had probably decided to let her sleep late and was already fixing breakfast. He could be so charming and thoughtful, she mused. But when she got to the kitchen, she found it empty. The house was completely silent. Had he left for work already? Surely he would have said goodbye.

Then she noticed a simple breakfast laid out for her on the counter, fresh melon, a muffin and a glass of juice. A carafe of coffee sat beside the plate along with a neatly folded note.

Tess grabbed the note, ready to read it, but a movement caught her eye and she stared out the kitchen windows into the backyard. A shadow darkened the concrete apron of the pool and Tess held her breath. He'd taken a morning swim. She slowly released her breath and walked toward the French doors that led out onto the terrace. Her head buzzed and her fingers went numb from clutching the note so tightly. In just a few minutes this would be all over. Her conscience would be clean.

With a shaky stride, Tess walked along the side of the pool, then turned around the corner of the house. But she stopped cold when she realized the shadow she had seen had not been caused by Drew.

"Lucy?"

Her sister spun around and dropped the open box of detergent she was holding. "Tess?"

Tess gasped. "What are *you* doing here?"

"What are *you* doing here?" Lucy countered.

"You first," Tess demanded, needing a few more minutes to formulate her story. She couldn't tell Lucy she'd spent the night in Drew's bed. But what could she tell her? Had Lucy noticed that Tess hadn't come home last night?

"How did you know where I was?" Lucy asked.

"I—I followed you," Tess said, improvising as she went along. "I had an early meeting and I was just getting back home when I saw you leave and I followed you. And it's a good thing I did!" she cried, wagging her finger. "I suspected you were up to no good. What are you doing, Luce? Besides trespassing."

Lucy's defiant expression softened, then crumbled. Tears swam in her eyes before tumbling down her cheeks. Her knees buckled and she sat down beside the pool with a bump. "Oh, Tess. I don't know. I'm just so miserable and I've tried so hard to get closure but—but it's not working."

Tess slowly crossed the flagstone walk to stand beside her sister. At one time, she would have shuffled the both of them away from this spot as fast as she could. But now, she really didn't care. If Drew walked in on them, then so be it. She was ready to face the truth and take the consequences. Anything would be better than this constant worry and nagging tension.

Nearly all her life, she'd been responsible for Lucy's happiness. And now she'd become involved with the man Lucy loved, then hated—a mistake guaranteed to add to her sister's distress. Her motives had been pure, at least at first. But would Lucy understand and forgive her? She bent down and patted her sister on the shoulder. "Honey, stop crying and tell me what you were planning to do."

"Detergent," she said, sobbing. "In the pool filter. Wh-when he comes home—suds all over the backyard."

Tess stifled a giggle. Of all Lucy's tricks, this one was quite clever. Still, she shouldn't be laughing. This whole mess had reached critical mass and it was time to put an end to it. "I'm glad I was here to stop you, Luce."

"I should have stopped a long time ago," Lucy said,

wiping her eyes with her fingers. "As soon as I realized that nothing will keep me from loving him. I still love him, Tess. And I don't think I can stop."

The words struck Tess like a blow to her heart. Her breath caught in her throat and tears burned at the corners of her eyes. Lucy couldn't still love Drew! She couldn't because *Tess* loved him! With all her heart and soul, she loved Drew Wyatt and, until this very moment, she'd been afraid to admit it to herself.

"I've thought about it for days," Lucy continued. "And last night, I made a decision. If this last try at closure didn't work, I was going to call him and tell him how I felt." Lucy looked up at Tess. "And then you appeared. It was like fate, Tess."

"It wasn't fate," she said softly.

But Lucy didn't hear her. Her sister was so wrapped up in her own thoughts that she couldn't see the pain etched across Tess's expression or hear the tiny moan that wrenched from Tess's throat.

"That's what I'm going to do. I'm going to call him and we're going to talk. Face-to-face."

"But don't you—"

"Stop!" Lucy cried, holding up her hand. "I'm not going to listen to you anymore. I don't want to live without him and I'm willing to do anything to win Andy back. And if you don't like that, too bad. It's my life and my future."

Tess closed her eyes and attempted to gain control of her emotions. Her sister's happiness was at stake. Could she stand in her way? Could Tess be so selfish as to put her own happiness before Lucy's? "Do you think Drew still feels the same way about you?"

She brushed a tear from her cheek. "Drew?" Lucy asked, her forehead creasing with confusion.

"I—I mean Andy," Tess said, not bothering to cover her mistake. Hell, she was beyond caring. Once Lucy found out the truth, she'd probably hate her anyway, so what was the difference? "Do you think that there's a chance he might want to resume your relationship?"

Lucy lifted her shoulders in a careless shrug. "I know I've been with a lot of men and I've made a lot of mistakes," she said. "But what we shared was special. I can't be wrong about that. I know he loves me, Tess."

"Then we should talk to him," Tess said. "Right now. Let's go find him."

"Oh, he left for work," her sister replied. "I waited outside the gate and I saw his car leave before I came in. Besides, I'm really not ready for that. I have to buy a new dress and get my hair done. I'm not going to take any chances."

Tess stood and dusted off her suit, then reached out and offered Lucy a hand. "Come on, then. Let's go home. We'll eat a huge breakfast and then I'll come shopping with you. We'll pick out the most gorgeous dress we can find. When Andy sees you, he won't be able to resist you."

They walked through the yard to the front driveway, Rufus falling into step beside them. He glanced up at Lucy, then woofed softly. But her sister ignored him and he nuzzled his wet nose beneath Tess's hand. When they reached the gate, Tess gave the dog a pat, then sent him away. But before she did, she held out the crumpled note. Rufus took it in his teeth.

"Go bury that in the garden," she murmured. "Bury it deep."

TESS HAD JUST STEPPED out of the shower when Lucy came running into her bedroom, her face flushed and her eyes bright. "He's here! Oh, God, Tess, he's here. He's coming up the walk. It's like destiny...or—or karma. I was going to call him and somehow he knew. Don't you see, Tess? This means we *are* meant for each other."

"Drew—I mean, Andy is here?" Tess slowly lowered herself to sit on the edge of the bed, emotion draining from her right along with the warmth from her body. Her head whirled and she felt frozen in time. The moment of truth had arrived and she was going to greet it with wet hair and chattering teeth.

"You have to go down and answer the door," Lucy instructed. "Tell him I'll be right down. I have to get ready. He can't see me like this." She rushed off to her own room, leaving Tess sitting in her threadbare chenille robe and her tattered slippers. Before she could even turn and reach for her clothes, the doorbell rang.

"Oh, hell," she muttered, burying her face in her hands. "What difference does it make? I could be dressed in a potato sack or a designer gown and it wouldn't change a thing. They're both going to hate me before the hour is over." Maybe a hair shirt would have been the appropriate attire, she mused, but she didn't have one in her closet.

Tess tugged at the tie to her robe and raked her fingers through her wet hair. Then, on shaky legs, she walked to the front door. The doorbell rang once more before she had the courage to place her hand on the knob. Drawing a long, calming breath, she turned the knob and threw the door open, ready to meet her fate.

A long sigh slipped from her throat as she met the gaze of a stranger. "Who are you?"

The man shoved his wire-rimmed glasses up the bridge of his nose and nervously straightened his tie. "That depends," the stranger said. "You're Tess, aren't you?"

She frowned, then stepped outside and looked around. "Where is Drew? Lucy said he was here."

"I—I'm Drew," the man said. "Actually, Lucy calls me Andy, but my real name is Elliot. Elliot Cosgrove. I'm Mr. Wyatt's business manager."

Tess pushed him aside and paced the length of the front porch. "Where is he? Why didn't he come himself? Is he that cowardly that he'd send his business manager to do his dirty work? I should have known."

"You don't understand," he said. "Mr. Wyatt isn't coming. Not the real Mr. Wyatt. That's why I'm here—to explain everything. You see, this is all my fault."

"What's your fault?" Tess demanded.

"Lucy thinks *I'm* Andrew Wyatt, and I've come to tell her the truth. And to beg her forgiveness."

She stopped pacing and stared at him. "Wait! What are you saying? Lucy's in love with *you?* She's not in love with Drew Wyatt?"

"That's one thing I'm not so sure about," he said, clasping his hands in front of him. "When she met me, I told her I was Andrew Wyatt. I was driving his car and living at his house. You see, I've never had much luck with women and Lucy is so beautiful. She thought I was Andrew Wyatt and I didn't tell her differently. And then, when you met Mr. Wyatt, I felt even worse. I knew, sooner or later, I'd have to come clean."

Tess felt her knees go weak. "Then—then my sister and I aren't in love with the same man?"

"Oh, no," Elliot said. "The same name, but not the same man."

An overwhelming sense of relief washed over Tess and emotion tightened her throat until she couldn't speak. All this time wasted, all the guilt, and it was completely unnecessary. Tess began to laugh, the anxiety pouring out of her with every giggle. She threw her arms around Elliot Cosgrove and hugged him. "Elliot, I'm so happy to meet you. You'll never know how—"

"Tess?"

Tess glanced over her shoulder to see Lucy staring at the two of them. "Oh, Lucy." She turned and gave her sister a hug as well. "This gentleman is here to see you. And I believe you two have a lot to talk about. I'll go make us some coffee."

Tess left Lucy and Elliot on the front porch. She didn't envy Elliot his news. Before he arrived, she'd had enough bad news to tell Lucy herself. But now, in the blink of an eye, the opening of a door, all of that had changed. She was free to love Drew Wyatt without remorse or regret. She could go to him and explain everything that had held her back. And he would understand and forgive. After all, she'd only been protecting her sister. He couldn't fault her for that.

As for Lucy, there would be no telling how she might react. She might be grateful to have the man she loved back in her life. Or she might be angry that she hadn't nabbed herself a rich boyfriend. She might even hate Tess for loving the man she thought *she* loved. But there was a very good chance that they both might come through this without a rift in their relationship. After all, the bottom line was, they were in love with completely different men.

Tess made a pot of coffee and settled herself at the breakfast table. By the time her sister wandered back into the kitchen, Tess had gulped down four cups of coffee and was prepared for the worst. The jitters had set in and she had occupied her shaky hands trying to piece together one of her sister's shattered Hummels. She looked up from her task to see Lucy standing in the doorway, her hand laced in Elliot's.

Tess smiled hesitantly. "Is everything all right?"

A bright light filled Lucy's expression and she nodded. "Everything is just fine," she said. "Andy—I mean, Elliot and I are getting married."

Tess jumped up from her chair, crossed the kitchen and threw her arms around Lucy's neck. "How did this happen?" she asked, glancing over at Elliot.

"I met Elliot at a symphony fund-raiser," Lucy explained. "He was there in place of his boss, Andrew Wyatt. And he saw me and fell in love at first sight. And I looked at the invitation he held in his hand and I jumped to the wrong conclusion. But that's all in the past now."

Tess stepped back and silently examined her future brother-in-law. "So you work for Andrew Wyatt," she said, curious as to how well Elliot knew the man she loved.

"We're business associates. And friends—I think. I take care of his house when he's out of town, watch his dog and—"

"Oh, his dog!" Lucy cried, turning to Elliot. "His purple dog. And all those other tricks I played on him. When I really meant to play those tricks on you. He'll be so angry when he finds out who did those things. He might fire you."

Tess grabbed her sister's hand. "Don't worry. I fixed Rufus before Drew had a chance to—"

"You fixed Rufus?" Elliot and Lucy asked in unison.

"It's a long story," Tess answered, shaking her head. "I'll explain it all later. For now, I need to talk to Drew. I need to tell him everything."

Lucy frowned. "But how do you know Andy—I mean, Drew?"

"Oh, I forgot to tell you," Elliot explained, anxious to illuminate Lucy. "Your sister and my boss are in love."

Lucy gasped, then turned her gaze to Tess. "You're in love with Andrew Wyatt? When did this happen?"

"No!" Tess cried. "I mean, yes, maybe I am in love with him. Luce, I know how this looks, but I didn't know who he was when I met him and he didn't know I was your sister. In fact, he doesn't even know you. And he doesn't know that—"

"Oh, he knows," Elliot said. "He's known everything for quite a while. I told him the whole story." As soon as the words slipped out, Elliot looked as if he wanted to swallow them up again.

"He knew?" Tess asked, her temper nearly choking her words. "The whole time? He knew that Lucy was really in love with you and that I was Lucy's sister?"

"Not—not the whole time," Elliot recanted. "But we found out about the stripper and the X-rated gifts and we put two and two together and figured you were behind all those tricks."

"But *I* was behind all those tricks!" Lucy said. "He can't blame Tess."

Tess slowly lowered herself back into her chair, the impact of Elliot's words sinking in. "How could I have been so stupid? This explains everything! All that false charm and fawning attention. He just sat back and watched me tie myself up in knots. Forcing me to chose between him and my sister when all the time I didn't need to make a choice at all."

"So Tess didn't know that Andy and Drew were different people," Lucy said. She turned to Tess with a befuddled frown. "And you fell in love with him thinking that he was the man I loved?"

Tess cursed softly. Finally, the truth was beginning to

seep through the romantic haze that had enveloped her sister. "No, not exactly. But that doesn't make any difference now! He *lied* to me! Maybe not directly, but he failed to tell me the whole truth."

Elliot cleared his throat. "Excuse me, Ms. Ryan, but aren't you guilty of that, too?"

"And what about *your* secrets, Mr. Cosgrove? People who live in glass houses…"

He looked properly chastened, a slow blush creeping up his cherubic cheeks. "When Mr. Wyatt finds out I came here, he's going to be very angry. He might even fire me. But I just couldn't stay away from my Lucy a minute longer. I had to tell her the truth." He glanced at his watch. "Now, I'd better get back to work and explain everything to Mr. Wyatt. He made me promise not to tell. He's not going to be happy that I broke his trust." He looked down into Lucy's eyes. "Dinner tonight?"

Tess's sister nodded, then reached up and wrapped her arms around Elliot's neck. She gave him a kiss that was enough to make both Elliot and Tess blush. When Lucy finally pulled back, Elliot's glasses had slipped down his nose and his cheeks had colored to fuchsia.

"I—I have to go now," he stammered.

He turned for the door, but Tess stopped him. "Wait," she said. "Before you leave, I want you to promise me something."

"Oh, I'll never do anything to hurt Lucy again," Elliot replied. "I'll make her the happiest woman in the—"

"I don't want you to tell Drew that we know," Tess interrupted. "As far as he's concerned, this visit never happened."

"I don't understand," Elliot said. "Everything is all right now."

"I don't understand, either," Lucy added, stamping her

foot and planting her fists on her waist. "Can somebody please explain. This is all too confusing!"

Tess stood up, a slow smile curling her lips. A perfect plan had come to her in a spark of divine inspiration. "Elliot, go back to work. And keep quiet. Lucy, you and I need to talk."

After Lucy escorted Elliot to the front door, she returned to the kitchen, confusion still creasing her forehead. She joined Tess at the table, pouring a cup of coffee for herself and wrapping her hands around the mug. A long silence settled between them as Lucy tried to sort out all that had happened. Tess knew how she felt. There were times when even she wasn't sure who knew what and when they knew it.

One thing Tess was certain of was that Lucy would figure everything out in time, but Tess couldn't afford to wait for that moment. "Remember that story I told you? About falling in love with my best friend's ex-boyfriend?"

Lucy nodded. "I was the best friend, wasn't I? And you thought Drew was my ex-boyfriend."

"I'm sorry, Luce. At first, I thought I could keep you from getting into trouble. And then I thought I might be able to make him pay for hurting you. And then...I fell in love with him. You have to know that it tore me up inside. I thought I was betraying you."

"But you weren't," Lucy said.

"I didn't know that! So it's still wrong."

Lucy reached out and covered Tess's hands with hers. "Drew Wyatt let you believe you were betraying me. He lied to you! He should be the one who is sorry."

A flood of affection overwhelmed Tess. When it came to their relationship, Lucy was loyal to a fault. Tess should have known that Lucy would forgive her anything.

"There is a way to make Drew pay for his deception," Tess said, "for putting me through such worry and guilt."

"What's your plan?" Lucy asked, her interest piqued.

Tess leaned back in her chair and took a long sip of coffee, relishing the telling of her plan as much as she would relish its execution. "First, I'm going to dump him. And then I'm going to commit murder."

Lucy's eyes went wide. "You're going to murder Andrew Wyatt?"

Tess shook her head and grinned. "Nope. I'm going to murder you."

DREW GLANCED over his shoulder and pulled his car into traffic. "I've made a decision, Elliot."

His business manager looked up from his open brief-case. "A decision, sir?" They had just finished the monthly budget meeting on the Gresham Park project and were on their way back to the office, weaving through stop-and-go traffic on the city streets.

"I've decided to put an end to these games with Tess Ryan. She refuses to tell me the truth, so I'm going to force the issue. I'll make her admit how she feels."

In Drew's mind flashed an image of Tess, lying in his bed, her hair mussed by slumber. He'd had all that he could handle that night, leaving her to sleep alone. But Drew knew that if he had crawled in beside her, he'd never be able to resist the temptation to touch her. Tess had become everything he wanted in a woman and it had taken all his control to maintain a safe distance.

He could only speculate what she'd come to tell him. He found out later that she'd stolen every pink flamingo from his lawyer's front yard. But she had arrived at his front door in the wee hours for another reason. Lying awake, with her in the next room, he'd convinced himself that she'd finally come to put an end to her charade. He'd run through the script in his head until he nearly had it perfect. She'd confess her complicity in all the petty acts of revenge, she'd ask his forgiveness. And then Drew would tell her that he'd never even met Lucy Ryan.

Drew sighed. There would come a time when she'd fall asleep in his arms every night and they'd wake up together each morning. He was determined to make that happen, at all costs. But after the little surprise she'd left at his house yesterday morning, Drew wondered if it would happen any time soon.

Elliot squirmed in his seat, an uneasy scowl on his face. "I don't think that's a very good idea, sir. All these secrets. The truth is getting harder and harder to find."

"Hey, I'm not the one perpetuating this situation. I got home yesterday to find my backyard filled with soapsuds. How do you think that happened?"

"Detergent in the pool filter?" Elliot mumbled.

Drew turned and stared at his business manager. "I never thought of that. Interesting. And how would you know that?"

Elliot fixed his attention on the traffic outside. "How do you feel about Tess Ryan, sir?"

"I love her," Drew said, gripping the wheel with white-knuckled hands. "I've loved her since the first time we met. That's the truth. But does she love me? I don't have a clue. And the hell if I'm going to hang my butt out there without knowing for sure."

Elliot cleared his throat. "Sometimes a guy has to hang his butt out there for love...sir."

Somehow, the statement seemed much more profound than it ought to. Elliot had hung it out there for love, pretending to be Drew, putting his job, his professional reputation, on the line for Lucy Ryan. But Drew wasn't quite that stupid. He wasn't willing to risk his butt, or his heart. Not on a woman who didn't return his feelings. "Even so, I called Tess and asked her to meet me at my office. I told her I needed to talk to her."

"You're going to ask her to marry you?"

Drew gasped and gaped at Elliot. "What? No, I'm not going to ask her to marry me."

"But you love her," Elliot said. "You should be together. Forever."

"We will be," Drew replied. "If and when she admits that *she* loves *me*."

"You could just ask her. I mean, what does it matter who says it first?"

Drew leaned back in the seat and drummed his fingers on the steering wheel. Elliot's suggestion was simple enough. But then, the guy didn't really know women, did he? Drew needed to play this very carefully. If Tess believed that he had dumped her sister, Lucy, then he was finally going to confirm those beliefs. If she loved him, she would admit it. And if she didn't, she'd leave him to Lucy.

Drew rubbed his forehead. At least, that's the way he thought he would play it. There were times when he felt as if he couldn't keep the situation straight in his head. Tess's truths and his truths and Lucy's truths ran together in his head until they were a confused muddle. Even Elliot had a pack of lies to his credit.

It would be so simple to wipe the slate clean, to start from the beginning. He could forgive Tess her mistakes and she could forgive Elliot his. Maybe Lucy and Elliot could even work their relationship out. This could all turn out for the best if Tess would just drop this facade and admit the truth.

He pulled the steering wheel to the left and turned into

the parking lot of his office. He noticed Tess's car parked in the visitor's spot near the door. He quickly pulled into the spot beside her, flipped off the ignition and hopped out of the car. Elliot hurried after him.

"Sir, don't you think it would be best to clear the air with Ms. Ryan? There's a lot to be said for clear air."

"Elliot, I know what I'm doing. This is the best way." He strode into the atrium lobby of the building and headed toward his suite of offices. Kim greeted him as he walked through the reception area, informing him that Tess Ryan was waiting in his office.

He walked in and found her perusing the photos on his wall. He'd collected pictures of all of his biggest projects. The wall always impressed his clients and he hoped Tess felt the same, though when she turned to face him, her expression was unreadable.

Her gaze fell on his face. "Why so serious?" she asked with a mock frown. "Don't tell me Mr. Lubich has struck again."

Drew stepped behind his desk and flipped through his messages. How could she ask him that with such a straight face? She knew the answer, but he wasn't going to give her the satisfaction of a reply. "I waited last night."

"Last night?" Tess asked.

"Dinner. At my place. The note I left for you?"

"Oh, the note," Tess said. "I didn't read it. I rushed out so fast that morning. I had to get to work. I'm sorry, I should have read it, but it just slipped my mind."

He studied her for a long moment and she returned his gaze with an attitude that looked like defiance. Was she angry at him? "You wanted to tell me something the other night. Before you fell asleep? What was it?"

Tess ran her fingers along the edge of his drawing board, studying the blueprint he had laid out there with a distracted stare. "Oh, nothing," she said, smiling. "Nothing important. Do you have anything important to tell me?"

"Actually, I do," Drew said, jumping at the convenient opening in the conversation. "I'm not sure you're going to like it."

"I probably won't," she said with a cool look. "But why don't you tell me anyway?"

"Well, it has to do with a woman. From my past."

"Your rubber dolly?"

Drew frowned. What had gotten into Tess? He'd seen her in myriad moods, but she'd never been so flippant and sarcastic. She seemed to be baiting him. But why? And why no reaction when he mentioned a woman from his past? "No," Drew continued. "Her name was...Lucy."

She was so composed, so unflappable, Drew mused. Her only response was a subtle lift of her eyebrow. "Lucy?"

"We were together before I met you. Then we split up, but I'm not sure I'm really over her."

For an instant, he thought he detected a trace of anger in her eyes, but she covered it with a benign smile. "You don't say! Well, that's a problem, isn't it? One man, two women. Good for you, bad for the women."

Suddenly, he felt as if he had just stepped out of a plane without a parachute, hurtling toward the ground at a terrifying speed. She wasn't reacting at all the way she was supposed to. In fact, they could have been discussing the weather, for all the emotion she invested in their conversation. Realization nagged at his brain. Maybe she didn't love him at all. "Tess, I don't feel right about it," he said, pressing on. "And that's why I have to see her again. I need to decide."

Her eyebrow arched. "Between the two of us? Tough decision."

"It would be easier if I knew your feelings," Drew suggested, choosing his tone carefully.

"Ah, my feelings." Tess smiled. "Well, I do have a few feelings now that you mention it."

"And what would they be?"

"I want to make your decision easy. I think you should go back to this Lucy person. You obviously love her. And who am I to stand in the way of true love? I'm sure she'd be happy to have you back."

Drew stifled a curse. Where had he lost control of this conversation? "But—but I'm not sure I love her," he said.

"Oh, but you probably do," she said, brushing aside his doubts with a wave of her hand. "Some women are impossible to forget."

The truth of her words hit him hard. Tess would be impossible to forget. She was also impossible to figure out! "So—so you're all right with this?" Drew said. "It's fine with you if I see this old girlfriend?"

She shrugged. "Of course. I have no claim on you. This—what was her name—Lucy? I'm sure Lucy's still madly in love with you. After all, a trustworthy and honest guy is hard to find. Believe me, I know."

"But what about us?"

"There is no us," Tess said, a cold edge in her voice. "It's obvious you've never forgotten Lucy. So I guess we need to say our goodbyes." She held out her hand. "It was nice knowing you, Drew."

Stunned, Drew took her fingers in his. "Tess, I'm not sure we should—"

"I'll have to be going now," she interrupted. "I've got to get back to work."

With that, she turned on her heel and hurried out of his office. He started after her, but then stopped when he reached the door. Elliot appeared at his side, watching Tess with a curious eye. "So, how did it go, sir? Did she admit that she loved you?"

Drew slowly shook his head, baffled. Somehow, this had turned out all wrong. Nothing had gone as he had planned. Nothing!

"Sir? Are you all right?"

"No, I'm not all right," he finally replied. "Tess Ryan just dumped me."

9

A SPRING STORM rumbled on the black horizon as Drew walked up to the front door of the dark and silent house. Flashes of lightning brightened the distant sky and a humid night wind rustled the live oaks that stood guard over the front yard. A sense of foreboding prickled the hairs on the back of his neck, but Drew wrote it off to the ominous forecast. Tornado weather always made him a little jumpy.

Tess had called him a half hour ago, her tone frantic, begging him to come to her home immediately. He hadn't expected to hear from her again, not so soon, and not with a middle-of-the-night invitation. After she had stalked out of his office, he had assumed they were through, at least from her point of view.

The past few weeks had been sheer misery. He'd been so lonely, so desperate to occupy his time with something other than thoughts of Tess that he'd begun to cultivate a relationship with Rufus. The dog had developed a grudging affection for Drew and had taken to sleeping at the foot of his bed. But there was no way Rufus could be a substitute for Tess.

He glanced up at the facade, its design like so many of the mansions in Buckhead. Maybe he'd been given another chance with her, perhaps she'd changed her mind. Just fifteen minutes before, he had awoken to the ring of his bedside phone. When he picked it up, his watch had read two in the morning. He'd thrown on a pair of jeans and a T-shirt and hopped into his car. Finding her house in the dark was nerve-racking, but when he got to the right address, he'd been surprised that she hadn't left a light burning for him.

Drew took the front-porch steps two at a time, rubbing his eyes to rid himself of the last traces of sleep. Something had upset Tess enough to call him and he was worried it was something serious, maybe a confrontation with her sister. After all, Tess still thought she was dating her sister's boyfriend. And Lucy didn't know any differently. He and Cosgrove were the only people who knew the real truth.

Just as he was about to knock, he noticed the door was open a crack. He gave it a push, then peered inside. "Tess? Tess, are you here?"

If she planned to tell him the truth, why hadn't she done it in his office that afternoon? Why call him at two in the morning and drag him over to a dark house? Or had she wanted her sister to be present for the big event?

In all honesty, Drew was looking forward to meeting Lucy Ryan. He wanted to get a good look at the woman who had caused all this trouble, the woman who had charmed Elliot, had set Tess on her path of vengeance and turned a potentially pleasant love affair into a tangle of lies and silly tricks.

He slowly made his way to the living room, bumping against furniture along the way, cursing at the dark. A bolt of lightning cracked the sky, flaring the windows that lined the walls. He caught a glimpse of a silhouette against one of the windows and he walked toward it. "Tess? Is that you?"

Another flash of lightning blazed, but the figure was gone. He must have imagined it. He got his bearings and walked toward the rear of the house. Something crunched under his foot and Drew bent down, searching the thick carpet with his hands. A shard of broken porcelain pricked his finger, drawing blood. "What the hell is—"

Panic rushed through him. Had someone broken into the house? Is that why Tess had called? Cursing, he fumbled to find a light switch. But when he flipped it, he discovered the power was out. "Tess! Tess, where are you?"

Why hadn't she called the police? Certainly they could have made it to the house faster than he had. Horrible images filled his mind, sending his panic into overdrive. Tess could be injured, maybe seriously. Fear clutched at his voice. "Tess, answer me."

"I'm right here." Her reply was soft, calm.

He snapped his head around at the sound. "Where are you?"

"Over here."

He moved in the direction of her voice, then nearly tripped over her. She sat on the floor, her back braced against a doorjamb. Drew bent down and squinted into the dark, trying to read the expression on her face, but the light was too dim. "Are you all right?"

"Not really," she said with a ragged sigh.

He cupped her cheek in his hand. "What happened here?"

She drew a shaky breath. "There was a fight. A big fight."

"With whom?"

Her hands searched the dark until she found the front of his T-shirt. She grabbed on tight and pulled him closer. "I didn't mean to," she said, desperation coloring her words. "I just wanted to explain and then we started to argue and things got out of hand."

"Who?" Drew demanded. "Who did you fight with?"

"Lucy!"

"Lucy?"

"You know—Lucy. Lucy Ryan Courault Battenfield Oleska. My sister and your ex-lover! The woman you decided you still loved."

"Tess, I—"

"I told her all about us, about the kisses and the touching, and she came after me. She was so angry, like the devil had gotten inside of her. I've never seen her like that. She screamed and she flailed and I was so frightened. I—I grabbed one of her Hummels—you know, those tiny little porcelain figurines. And I threw it at her."

Drew sat down beside and took her hand in his. "Tess, I'm sorry. I didn't ever think this would get so out of hand. I—"

"I killed her," Tess said, her voice flat and emotionless. "I hit her on the head with that Hummel and she went down like tall timber. Those little suckers are heavy."

Drew's breath froze in his throat. "What?" he gasped. "What did you say?"

"Hummels are heavy," Tess repeated. "Funny, it didn't break when it hit her head, just when it hit the floor."

"Not the Hummels, Tess! What did you say about Lucy?"

"Oh, I killed her. At least, I think I did."

Drew scrambled to his feet. "Where is she, Tess? Did you call an ambulance? We need to call the police."

"She wasn't breathing. I'm pretty sure she was dead. So I dragged her out to the garden and I dug a hole and I buried her. Right under the rose arbor. I—I think she was dead. I mean, I'm not a doctor, but she wasn't moving."

He reached down and yanked her to her feet, his mind racing. "Good Lord, Tess. What have you done? This was all a mistake. It wasn't meant to go this far. I never meant—"

"I dug the hole deep," Tess said in a detached voice. "But maybe I shouldn't have covered her with all that dirt."

"Show me where!" he cried. "It might not be too late. She might still be alive. Damn it, Tess, show me where you buried your sister."

He followed her through the kitchen and out into the rear garden. Like so many of the old homes in Buckhead, this one featured a huge backyard, deep enough for a formal Southern garden. He'd never be able to find the spot on his own. He prayed that Tess would be able to remember, that it wouldn't be too late for her sister.

It was pitch-black outside, the storm clouds scudding over the full moon. His earlier feeling of foreboding suddenly made sense—the dark house, the open door, the broken porcelain. Hell, he should have know something was wrong as soon as Tess called. But he never imagined this!

Drew cursed and, with every heartbeat, condemned himself for his actions. How could he have been so manipulative? Why hadn't he seen what his lies might do? Love was a powerful emotion; it made people do irrational things. He saw it on the news every night, murder and love intertwined, yet he'd treated both Tess and Lucy like pawns in his sick little game.

He was as responsible for this tragedy as Tess was. If it hadn't been for him, none of this would have happened. And if Lucy was really dead, if Tess had committed murder, then Drew was prepared to suffer the consequences right alongside her. He'd confess his complicity to the police and accept whatever punishment he deserved.

"Here," Tess said, pointing to a patch of overturned earth. "This is where I put her."

Drew snatched up a nearby shovel and began to dig, his heart slamming against his chest, his breath coming in short gasps. "How deep?" he asked as he heaved a shovelful of dirt over his shoulder.

"Pretty deep," Tess said, squatting to watch him. "Maybe we should just leave her there. She'll be all dirty."

"Damn it, Tess. What's gotten into you? She could still be alive and you're acting like you don't even care."

"But you do," she said. "You're in love with Lucy. That's why you're trying to save her."

He slammed the shovel into the soft dirt, the hole deepening. "I don't even know your sister!" he said, the guilt like a bitter pill in his mouth. "Lucy was in love with my business manager. He told her he was me and, after he broke up with her, you started your little acts of revenge. I just wanted to get you to confess, that's why I told you I was going back to Lucy. I never thought—"

A slow realization seeped into Drew's mind and he paused in his task. Something wasn't right here. The tone of Tess's voice, the subtle hint of humor in her words, as if she was smiling in the dark. His grip tightened on the shovel and he looked up.

"You think that's deep enough, Luce?" Tess's voice rang loud and clear in the night. Drew, now nearly knee-deep, noticed another figure illuminated by the sporadic flashes of lightning on the horizon. A woman, nearly the same height as Tess and sharing her dark hair and slender limbs, stood beside her.

"I don't know," the woman said. "Daddy likes to plant his rosebushes deep. Maybe he should dig a little more."

A slow, sick feeling hit him, twisting at his gut. At the same time, a flashlight flipped on and glared in his eyes. He held up his hand, tossing the shovel to the ground.

"Does he look sorry enough, Luce? After all, he's got a lot to be sorry for. He's known the truth for days. But he didn't speak up. He decided to play a little game of his own." Tess bent down, shifting the light from his eyes so he could see her face.

Drew shook his head in disbelief. "What about *your* little tricks, Tess?"

"My tricks," Lucy interjected. "They were all mine. Tess tried to fix them but she didn't always get there in time. She was just protecting me. And all because *your* business manager decided to pretend to be you! So don't you blame her for anything. She's a good sister and I love her!" With that, Lucy turned and walked toward the house.

Tess pushed to her feet. "I guess this puts an end to my short career in the revenge business." She looked up at the sky, then back at him. "I think you better get out of that hole. It's about to rain."

With that, she spun on her heel and stalked off, leaving him standing in the hole he'd dug for himself. Just when Drew didn't think things could get any worse, the skies opened up and the rain came down in sheets, turning his hole into a growing pool of muddy water and muck.

"Well, this is a fine mess you've gotten yourself into," Drew muttered. He struggled to crawl out of the hole, then rolled over on his back and let the rain wash over his face.

There were times—not many, but certainly more than a few—when he regretted ever setting eyes on Tess Ryan.

"YOU LOOK SO PRETTY," Tess said, reaching up to brush an errant strand of hair from Lucy's face. She straightened the fashionable hat and veil, then stepped back.

Her sister smiled, tears swimming in her eyes. "I'm so happy, Tess." Lucy glanced down at the sophisticated suit she wore. "Do you think it's all right that I wear white? This is my fourth wedding, after all. I'm what you'd call a veteran. Maybe I should be wearing camouflage."

"It's the first time I've ever seen you as a bride. And my first time as a maid of honor." Tess glanced through the ornately carved doors into the tiny flower-filled chapel. "It's going to be a lovely wedding. I just wish Daddy could be here to give away the bride."

"He'll be able to give you away at your wedding," Lucy said.

Tess knew the prospect of that was dim and growing dimmer by the second. "I wouldn't count on that. This is my first and last trip down the aisle."

Lucy's eyes shifted and she stared over Tess's right shoulder. "You never know what might happen. Things could work out."

Tess followed her gaze to see Drew entering the chapel at Elliot's side. Her heart skipped and a tiny thrill shot through her. It had only been a few weeks since she'd seen him last, standing in that muddy hole, but it seemed like forever. He was dressed in a finely tailored suit that fit him to perfection, the jacket emphasizing his broad shoulders. But he looked a little thinner, as if he hadn't been eating.

He raked his hands through his windblown hair and her fingers clenched as she remembered the feel of it, soft between her fingers. Suddenly, everything came rushing back to her with absolute clarity—the feel of his lips on hers, the sound of his voice, the incredible blue of his eyes. How had it gone so wrong?

She scolded herself silently, reining in her runaway thoughts. "What's *he* doing here?"

Lucy winced, then shot Tess an apologetic smile. "He's Elliot's best man. I knew if I told you, you wouldn't come. And I just had to have you here, Tess. I couldn't get married without you. Please don't be mad."

Tess sighed, then looked away as he turned in her direction. She could sense him staring at her, his eyes slowly drifting over her body like a silent caress. "It's all right. I suppose we can put our differences aside for just one day."

Lucy grabbed Tess and kissed her on the cheek. "Thank you. Now, come on, it's time to go inside. I'm getting married for the last time in my life."

Tess followed her sister and Elliot to the altar of the chapel. Drew fell into step right behind her. The minister waited for them, dressed in a white robe. When they reached the front of the church, she took her place to the left of Lucy.

Tess didn't risk a glance at Drew until the minister began to speak. Slowly, she raised her eyes from her tiny bouquet of lilies. When she found him staring at her again, she looked away. A warm blush crept up her cheeks.

How could he still affect her so strongly? After all he'd done, she should hate him. But every time she tried to work up feelings of anger and disgust, they melted beneath the onslaught of her memories. Memories of his touch, of his kisses. Memories of what might have been.

If she could just get through the next thirty minutes, she'd never have to see him again. But that thought was almost too difficult to imagine. From the first time she'd met him, she'd always secretly hoped he would have a spot in her future. Though she tried to ignore those thoughts, they'd always been there. Now, standing in a church in the midst of a wedding, she realized that this had been part of her picture, too—only she and Drew had been the bride and groom.

She listened halfheartedly as Lucy and Elliot exchanged their vows, the words of everlasting love and commitment like daggers to her heart. Would she ever find a man to share her life? Would there ever come a time when she could forget the past and trust in love?

This time when Tess looked up, she met Drew's eyes without flinching. Their gazes locked and she drew in a soft breath. What she saw there in the blue depths caused her heart to flutter, then stop for an instant. It was as if she could see past all that had happened, all that stood between them, right into his soul. She saw regret and need, desire and frustration. And though he'd never said the words, in that instant she saw a deeper truth in his eyes. He loved her.

"I now pronounce you husband and wife. You may kiss your bride."

Lucy handed Tess her flowers, startling her back to reality. With an embarrassed smile, Tess fumbled with the bouquet, then watched her sister throw her arms around Elliot and kiss him passionately. At first, Elliot's reserved nature prevented him from responding in kind, but then he pushed it aside and kissed Lucy with equal enthusiasm.

Congratulations were exchanged all around with Elliot giving Tess a hug and Drew offering the same to Lucy. But as soon as Drew moved toward her, Tess stepped back and occupied herself with plucking at the ribbons in Lucy's bouquet. He would have hugged her, maybe even kissed her, but she couldn't let that happen. Tess knew as soon as he touched her, her resolve would disappear and she'd be lost in his arms.

Finally, Lucy grabbed her bouquet and hurried with Elliot to the doors of the chapel. Turning back to wave, she wound up, then threw the flowers in Tess's direction with the practiced aim and velocity of a Major League pitcher. The flowers hit Tess in the face, then dropped into her hands.

And then, the newlyweds were gone, rushing off to a week-long honeymoon in Bermuda. The course of true love never did run smoothly, but Tess believed that Lucy might finally make a success of marriage.

Tess stood in the same spot for a long time, the bouquet tucked under her chin, tears pressing at the corners of her eyes. The chapel grew silent and the minister retired to his office.

"I guess you're next," Drew said with a soft chuckle.

Tess jumped, forgetting that he was still standing beside her. "I—I don't think so. It's just a silly wedding superstition."

"So you've sworn off men? I hope I'm not to blame for that."

"They're nothing but trouble. You only reinforced what I already knew."

Drew shook his head. "You shouldn't write off the barrel just because of one bad apple." He paused and stared down the empty aisle of the chapel. "I envy Elliot," he murmured. "He's a lucky guy. He's found a woman to love him, a woman to spend his life with…someone to trust with his heart. That's exactly what I've been looking for." He drew a long breath. "Tess, I know what I did was wrong, but I—"

She held up her hand to silence him. "I really don't want to talk about it."

He took her fingers in his and placed a kiss in the center of her palm, his lips sending a pulsing current of sensation through her limbs. "But I do. We can't go on like this. We have to talk. We have to try to straighten this out."

"Do you really think we can? We've made such a mess of it. It's like a ball of string with knots and twists and snarls. When we finally untangle it, there'll be nothing left. Nothing in the center."

"You can't believe that."

"I don't know what I believe," she said. "Except that my life is calm and orderly now. I have my career and I keep busy and—"

"And what about the nights, Tess? When you're lying all alone in your bed. What do you think about? Do you know what I think about?"

"I don't think I want to know what you think about."

"I think about you. About how good it was, even in the midst of all the chaos we created. I think about how much I wanted to hold you that night you slept in my bed and how I forced myself to sleep in another bed because I knew, someday, you'd be in my arms for good. I knew it like I knew my own name. And I think about how this should have been our wedding, that we should be walking out of this chapel and into the rest of our lives together."

"And do you think about lying to me?"

"I'm sorry for that. It was stupid, but I did it for what I thought was a good reason. I wanted to know how you really felt about me. I wanted to be sure. I couldn't trust my feelings for you."

"Well, now you are sure. You know exactly how I feel."

She started toward the doors of the chapel, but Drew grabbed her arm and gently turned her back around. "I'm not going to give up on us, Tess."

"And I'm not going to change my mind."

She pulled her arm from his grip and with trembling knees walked down the aisle and out of the chapel. This was all for the better. After all that had passed between them, there was no way to go back to the beginning. The sooner she put Drew Wyatt in the past, the sooner she could get on with her life.

"Tess? Tess, are you home? We're back!"

Lucy's voice echoed through the house and Tess sighed softly. It had been so quiet for the past week she had nearly forgotten how nice it was to have someone to talk to. Even though Lucy could be a pain at times, she had been an amusing roommate and a wonderful confidante.

"Tess, there's a For Sale sign in the front yard. What's going on? Tess, where are you?"

If she just lay still, maybe Lucy wouldn't find her. Maybe she and Elliot would leave and Tess wouldn't have to listen to how wonderful their honeymoon had been, how much they loved each other and how blissfully happy they were. Not that she would begrudge her sister any of those things, but she'd been in a blue funk ever since the wedding—ever since she'd seen Drew, to be more precise.

How many times had she replayed Drew's words to her, evaluating and reevaluating the truth in them? He'd said everything she wanted to hear, but still, she couldn't trust herself to believe him. Maybe there had been too much deceit between them to go back. Or maybe she just didn't believe that a man like Drew could love her.

She'd nearly convinced herself that she was better off without him. She could almost get through an entire day without thinking of him. The nights were still difficult, sitting alone at the dinner table, lying in bed with a book, closing her eyes to sleep. He invaded her thoughts and dominated her dreams and she woke up nearly every morning with the same unfulfilled longing and aching emptiness.

Tess kicked at the underside of her bed. It really wasn't bad here in the dark among the dustballs. There was a certain tranquillity that Lucy had discovered long ago. It was quiet and peaceful and the world seemed to fade away in this cramped space. All she could hear was her own breathing and she could barely see her hands in front of her face.

But even the darkness couldn't banish his image from her brain. She cursed softly. It wouldn't do to dwell on him now. She needed a bright expression and a happy attitude for Lucy. Tess pasted a smile on her face, testing a cheerful demeanor. It was then she realized that she hadn't smiled in a week, not since she'd waved goodbye to her sister at the chapel and walked away from Drew.

A soft light filtered beneath the bed and Tess turned to see Lucy peering beneath the dust ruffle. "Hi," she said. "You're back."

"What are you doing under there, Tess?"

"I just thought I'd give it a try," she replied. "It's not too bad."

"Will you come out and say hi to Elliot? He's been worried about you."

Tess shook her head. "I think I want to stay here for just a little while longer if that's all right."

Lucy lay down on the floor and slid under the bed until she lay next to Tess. She reached above her head and produced a small package from behind the headboard. "Twinkies," she said. "You want one?"

"You hide food under my bed?"

"Sometimes I get hungry. Junk food always went with

the ambience under here. I've also got some Oreos around here somewhere."

"I'm not hungry, Luce."

Lucy looked over at her. "Are you still upset about Drew? I know it was hard for you at the wedding, but I thought if the two of you had a chance to talk, you might—"

"I try not to think about him."

"But it's not working, is it?" Lucy said.

Tess sighed, a sudden flood of emotion bringing tears to her eyes. "No."

"I know something that will help you forget."

"What's that?"

"Closure," Lucy said. "I hear it's an actual psychological theory."

A giggle burst from Tess's throat. Her tears turned into gales of laughter as she and Lucy considered the absurdity of her words. This is where it had all started such a short time ago. And look what had happened to them since then. Lucy had found a husband. Tess had fallen in—and out—of love. They both were forever changed. And now their roles had been reversed. *Lucy* was consoling *Tess* over a broken romance.

"What are you going to do?" Lucy asked.

"I'm thinking of moving. Maybe to Washington, D.C. I've got some contacts through Daddy. Marceline Lavery's sister is married to a senator and she says there would be plenty of business for me there. I just want to start over fresh, someplace where there are no bad memories."

"But you can't move!" Lucy cried, reaching out to grab her hand. "I need you here."

"Luce, you have Elliot now."

"But you're my sister. I've known you forever. Elliot's sweet but he's still a man."

"Now that you're settled, Dad and Rona want to sell the house. It's a good time for a change," Tess said.

"Elliot says Drew is talking about the same thing. He's thinking about taking a project in Italy. Some new art museum in Milan. He's going to be gone for months. He'll probably forget you, being around all those lusty Italian women."

"That's good," she said, trying to hide the pain in her voice. "See, he's moving on with his life. So should I."

"Oh, Tess, you are such a fool. Anyone can see that you love the man. And, according to Elliot, he loves you. Stop being so stubborn!"

"Luce, I appreciate your advice, but I need to work through this on my own. I'll be all right, I promise." She drew a deep breath. "Now, why don't we go see how Elliot's doing? I want to hear all about your honeymoon. Did you bring me a present?"

That was all it took to change the subject. As they crawled out from beneath the bed, Lucy chattered on about their trip to Bermuda. But Tess couldn't concentrate on her sister's stories. Her mind kept returning to Drew and to Elliot's claim that he loved her.

She'd seen it in his eyes at Lucy's wedding, but she'd refused to trust her feelings. Letting herself believe was just too risky. But wasn't a future with Drew worth some risk? After all, what did she have to lose?

She'd already lost her heart. It couldn't get much worse than that.

THE CELEBRATION BEGAN early at Wyatt and Associates. As soon as Drew received the call from the civic center committee, he popped the champagne and passed out chocolate cigars. Though it was only noon, Drew decided that he needed a little levity in his life. He hadn't really felt happy since the last time he'd looked into Tess Ryan's eyes—nearly a month ago by his calendar.

But he'd made a vow to forget her and he'd done his best to stick to it. He'd thrown himself into his work, spending nearly every waking hour at the office, only going home when he was so exhausted he could do nothing more than tumble into bed and pass a dreamless night.

Still, there wasn't an hour of the day in which he didn't think of Tess, didn't wonder what she was doing, how she was feeling. He had tried to pump Elliot for information, but his business manager was notoriously closemouthed. One- or two-word answers were all that Elliot would allow. Good. Fine. Well. Very busy. That was the extent of the news of Tess Ryan.

Drew held up his champagne flute and glanced around the room at his staff. "Here's to a lot of hard work and fine talent. We couldn't have won this project without each and every one of you. It's time to celebrate now. But tomorrow, we'll help this city build a new civic center."

Everyone broke into a round of self-congratulatory applause, slapping each other on the back and toasting their success. Though Drew felt satisfied with the win, he couldn't seem to work up much enthusiasm for a party. He stepped back to his office door and watched the festivities from the sidelines, his shoulder braced on the doorjamb.

The door to the reception area opened and a slender figure stepped inside, catching his eye. For a moment, Drew's breath froze as he recognized long, dark hair and slender limbs, a pretty profile. But then he realized that it wasn't Tess walking into his office, but her sister, Lucy. He slowly released his pent-up breath then scolded himself silently.

The longer he went without seeing Tess, the more he began to see her likeness in Lucy. Lucy often stopped into the office around the lunch hour, anxious to see her new husband, still enjoying their honeymoon. She spotted Elliot in a small group of employees and made her way over to him. Drew chuckled as she gave Cosgrove a hug and a chaste peck on the cheek. At one time, Elliot would have been mortified by such a public display of affection. Now he took it in stride.

Drew wondered if Elliot knew how damn lucky he was. A loving wife. The chance to have a family. He and Lucy had already decided to build a new home for themselves, a project that Drew had promised to design for them. He thought about his own house, how empty it still felt.

He turned away from the celebration and stepped inside his office. Blueprints and small-scale models littered his desk and he brushed aside a bid proposal and sat down at his drawing board. He'd never expected to get the civic center project, especially after the impromptu entertainment the committee had enjoyed in his reception area. In fact, he'd accepted the project in Milan as a contingency, partly to make up for the anticipated loss and partly to get away from Atlanta for a while.

But now, with both projects secured, Drew realized that the next six months were going to be a torture of transatlantic flights and strange hotel rooms. "Maybe that's what I need," he murmured. "More work."

"All work and no play make Drew a very grumpy man."

Drew turned in his chair to see Lucy standing in the doorway. He smiled. She was almost as pretty as Tess, but in his eyes, the older sister was the true beauty of the family. "Has Elliot been complaining again?"

Lucy shook her head and stepped inside. "You know my husband. He loves his work."

"We all do," Drew said.

She picked up a model and studied it, then carefully placed it back on his desk. "But there's more to life than just work, don't you agree?"

Drew sighed and busied himself with straightening out the pile of blueprints on his board. "Right now, that's about it for me. With the civic center project and the deal in Milan, I don't have much time for anything else."

"That's a very convenient excuse, Drew Wyatt," Lucy said, fixing her gaze on him. "And some people might buy it. But I don't believe you for a second."

A silence grew between them, the unasked questions hanging like dark clouds over their heads. "How is Tess?" he finally asked. "I can never seem to get much out of that husband of yours."

"She's trying to put on a happy face. But she's been spending a lot of time under her bed."

Drew blinked in confusion and Lucy smiled ruefully. "It's an old family tradition. Some folks sleep under the front porch when it's hot out, Tess and I crawl under the bed when we're sad or depressed. It's cheaper than Prozac.''

"How much time is she spending under the bed?" Drew asked.

"I've found her there three times in the past week. I think she's getting a little worried about the move."

He sat up straight. "The move?"

"Didn't Elliot tell you? She's thinking of moving to Washington, D.C. She's got some contacts there, and with my father being in the diplomatic corps, she feels that she can build a good clientele pretty quickly."

The news hit Drew like a runaway freight train. A knot of frustration tightened in his gut and he cursed inwardly. "No," he murmured. "Elliot didn't tell me. When is she leaving?"

"Soon," Lucy said. "The house is up for sale. So I guess if you're going to try to stop her, Andrew Wyatt, you had better get to it."

"Does she want to be stopped?"

Lucy walked toward him, then reached down and took his hands in hers. "If you're asking me if she loves you, I think she does. If you're asking me if she'll admit that she loves you, that's a different story. Tess has watched me mess up my love life for so many years, I'm not sure that she'd recognize true love if it dropped out of the sky and hit her on the head."

He studied her slender fingers, so much like Tess's. Yet there was no trace of the electricity he felt when he touched Tess. He cared for Lucy, but only because she meant so much to Tess. "I can't force her to feel something she doesn't feel."

"And how do *you* feel?"

Drew stood, then paced the confines of his office. "Do you even need to ask? The minute I met Tess, I fell in love with her. Even when I thought she was trying to drive me crazy with all those silly tricks, I loved her. And now that I've lost her, I'm in the impossible situation of loving her even more.''

''You haven't lost her yet,'' Lucy said. ''You must have shared something good. There have to be some special memories left that you can build on. Maybe you just need to remind her of that.''

Drew flopped back down in his chair and crossed his arms over his chest. If only it was that easy. When *he* thought about Tess, he never thought about the lies. Memories of all the bad had dissolved from his mind the moment he admitted he still loved her. But he knew that the lies had cut her deep, that her belief in him had been sorely shaken. And he'd done it all for his stupid pride, the pride that couldn't allow him to love without first being loved in return.

Tess had done nothing wrong. She had tried to help her sister through a difficult time, tried to protect Lucy from herself and her anger. And when Lucy lashed out, Tess did her best to protect her intended victim. Looking back on it now, Drew should have known that Tess could never deliberately hurt him. She didn't have it in her to be vindictive or conniving or coldhearted. She'd done it all to make life easier for someone she loved.

Tess was loyal and compassionate and tenacious, exactly the qualities that had attracted him in the first place. So why had he chosen to punish her for that? Maybe he wasn't punishing her at all. Perhaps he was condemning himself. He'd resolved to fall in love, thinking it would all be so simple. And when things didn't go as smoothly as he planned, he looked for someone to blame. Who better than Tess?

''Drew, you're the only one that can make her stay.

I've tried, but she doesn't think I need her anymore. And Tess really needs to be needed.'' Lucy paused. ''Make her remember. Show her that it wasn't all bad. I'm counting on you.''

With that, Lucy bent over and dropped a quick kiss on his cheek before she walked out of his office. Drew let her suggestion run through his mind again and again. With it, came images of his time with Tess. The alley behind the art museum where they'd danced together. Their evening at the Tiki Palace. The picnic high above the city. Even that silly hole he'd dug in her backyard made him smile.

Lucy was right. There were plenty of good things left from their time together. And if he could make Tess see that, then there would be plenty more to come. Now, all he had to do was figure out a way to make Tess remember.

THE DAY HAD BEEN FILLED with loose ends and boxes, goodbyes and best wishes. In preparation for her move to Washington, Tess had made final arrangements to sublet her office space and store her belongings. She had finished her last event the previous night and had turned all her future events over to Clarise. Now there was nothing left to do but take a long, hot shower and get a good night's rest.

She wasn't scheduled to leave for another week, but Tess needed the extra time to wrap up details on the care and sale of her parents' home. There was the gardener to pay and the cleaners to hire, bills to transfer and mementos to pack. The real estate agent had scheduled an open house for tomorrow and Tess wanted to be sure everything went smoothly. Though the house hadn't sold yet, the agent had assured Tess that it wouldn't be on the market much longer.

So many changes, Tess mused. And all happening so quickly. A few months ago, she thought her life—her future—was here in Atlanta. Her business had taken off and she'd had more work that she could possibly handle. Everything was perfect—or so she'd thought.

In truth, Tess had been going through the motions. Her life had become ordinary, an endless cycle of work and sleep that had given her no chance for a personal life. Until she'd met Drew Wyatt, she'd never realized how empty it all was. And then, suddenly, he had filled her days and nights with anxiety and desire, frustration and fantasy. She felt emotions that she hadn't even known existed. And she wanted to feel that again.

It was time to stop playing it safe. She'd spent her whole life in Atlanta, never venturing far from home. Her career had been nothing but an extension of her childhood, carefully planning the happiness of others, standing on the sidelines while her own happiness suffered. She'd even kept herself from loving Drew because she felt responsible for Lucy's happiness.

She needed a change, an earthshaking, routine-breaking alteration in the course of her life. Happiness was out there somewhere. If she didn't find it in Washington, she'd move on and look for it somewhere else. The one thing she did know was that she wouldn't find it here.

Tess was beginning to feel more and more like Lucy. She'd tossed aside her practical nature and looked to her emotions for guidance. As long as she worked in Atlanta, she would risk bumping into Drew and she knew she couldn't live with that risk. Lucy had accused her of running away from her problems, but Tess had preferred to think of her decision as a positive step toward her future happiness. Closure, perhaps.

Tess pulled her car into the driveway of the house just as the sun was setting. She glanced at the For Sale sign planted near the curb. Grass sprung up around the sign and she made a mental note to call the gardener. But as her gaze took in the wide front lawn, she gasped. A flood of memories assailed her mind and Tess pulled the car to a stop, the brakes screeching.

The entire yard was filled with pink flamingos! They were everywhere, hundreds of them. Who had—Tess sighed and shook her head. Who else would have pulled a trick like this? Drew! But why? After all this time, he couldn't still be holding a grudge, could he?

Tess climbed out of the car and slammed the door. Well, she wasn't going to react. She wasn't going to give him the satisfaction of getting angry. She'd just pretend that the flamingos weren't even there. Tess frowned. She might be able to ignore them, but the real estate agent wouldn't be so blind, nor would her clients. With a groan, Tess hurried across the lawn and began to pluck the birds out of the grass.

A group of neighbors gathered at the curb and watched her with undisguised curiosity. Cars stopped and honked and a few people even took pictures. One didn't usually see tacky lawn ornaments in Buckhead and it caused about as much of a stir as an alien invasion, though they all seemed to appreciate the humor in the situation.

As an experienced plastic-bird plucker, Tess had cleared nearly half the lawn when a strange sports car pulled up the driveway and parked behind her Toyota. A tall, muscular man climbed out, then shut the driver's door. He leaned back and watched her as she dropped the birds on the grass before he approached. Tess didn't recognize him, though he wore a work shirt with his name embroidered above the pocket.

"Are you Tess Ryan?"

She nodded. "Are you from the cleaning service?"

He grinned, shook his head, then leaned inside the open car window and cranked up the stereo. The Village People filled the air, the deep, thudding sounds of "YMCA" blaring through the air. Tess gasped as the man ripped off his shirt and began to dance in front of her. His belt came off slowly, but in one quick tug, his jeans were history. He tossed them in her direction and they hit her on the chest before dropping to the ground.

Tess glanced over to see her neighbors gaping at the scene. They seemed to find the stranger much more interesting than a bunch of plastic birds, and some of the ladies had already started up the driveway to get a closer look. The flamingos had been bad enough, but this was going way too far! Drew was taunting her, bringing up old offenses that she'd managed to put behind her. How could he do this to her? Was he trying to make her angry?

Moments later, to Tess's great relief, the stripper finished his dance. Dressed only in a male version of a G-string, he sauntered over and pulled a small envelope from the waistband. "There'll be a limo here in a half hour," he said. "Hope you have a nice evening, miss."

Tess watched him get in the car and drive off, then turned to her neighbors. "You can go home now," she called. "The show is over."

She glanced down at the note, then back at the flamingos still left standing on the lawn. Was the note another trick, another attempt to prick her conscience? Tess slowly unfolded it, then drew a deep breath before she read it.

"It wasn't all bad, was it?" she read out loud. Tess blinked, tears pushing at the corners of her eyes. She slowly drew her fingers over his handwriting. He wasn't angry. The flamingos and the stripper weren't meant to taunt her, but to remind her. To make her laugh. And she hadn't laughed in such a long, long time.

A tiny smile quirked at the corners of her mouth and she sighed. "No, it wasn't all bad." But was there enough good left over for her to forgive him?

THE LIMOUSINE ARRIVED exactly thirty minutes after the stripper left. Tess spent twenty-nine minutes in front of her closet trying to figure out what to wear. She would have had a better chance of choosing wisely had she known what was in store for her, but Drew's note revealed nothing.

"Closure," she murmured. That was what this would be. A nice little punctuation at the end of their very...odd relationship. Apologies would be made and goodbyes would be exchanged. Maybe she'd even have a chance to explain a few misunderstandings. And then she would go off to Washington without leaving any regrets behind. But what did one wear to a closure?

The limo driver honked again and Tess jumped. With a soft oath, she grabbed a slim navy blue sheath. The dress had a simple, conservative neckline and a provocative slit up the thigh. She'd say goodbye but she'd leave him something to remember.

Tess had just thirty seconds to dash on some makeup, dig up her pearls from the bottom of her jewelry box and slip on her shoes. She raced downstairs and out the front door into the twilight of a perfect spring evening. The driver, dressed in a tidy uniform, opened the car door for her and helped her inside.

It wasn't until he pulled out into the road that she realized what she was doing. She was going to see Drew!

They would come face-to-face for the first time in over a month. She would have to look past those beautiful blue eyes, ignore that handsome profile and steel her shaky resolve. And if he touched her, even casually or unintentionally, there was no telling what might happen.

"Driver!" she called. Tess slid off the seat and pounded on the sliding window behind the chauffeur. "Driver, I need to talk to you."

The window lowered with a soft whir. "Is there something wrong, ma'am?"

"I want to go home," Tess said. "Now. Turn the car around and take me home."

"I'm afraid I can't do that," the driver said with a frown.

"What do you mean?" Tess asked, gripping the edge of the window. "You can't take me where I don't want to go! That's—that's kidnapping."

"We'll be there shortly, ma'am. If you want to leave once Mr. Wyatt talks to you, then I'll be happy to take you home."

Tess flopped back against the soft leather seat and watched the scenery pass by the tinted windows. What had possessed her to get into this car? What had she been thinking? Experience should have told her that seeing Drew again wouldn't be easy. But in the rush of the moment, with the limo waiting, she'd forgotten the kind of effect he could have on her.

What if he planned more than just an apology and a goodbye? Could she maintain her resolve and keep her distance? Good grief, she'd have to! She'd closed up her business, she'd packed her belongings and she was about to start a new life in a different city. She couldn't consider starting things up with him again.

"This will be closure," she assured herself, "and nothing more."

Twenty minutes later, to Tess's surprise, the limousine pulled up in front of the art museum. The driver helped her out of the car then escorted her to the front entrance where a security guard waited. The guard opened the door and ushered her inside.

The interior of the museum was dim and silent, the only sounds coming from the echo of their footsteps on the marble floors. Tess followed behind the guard, hoping that he'd pass a rest room where she might pause and soothe her nerves. But to her surprise, he led her through the cavernous reception hall and into the kitchen.

"What are we doing here?" she asked.

"Mr. Wyatt is waiting for you," the guard replied.

"In the kitchen?"

"No, ma'am. In the alley."

He opened the rear entrance and Tess stepped through the doorway. Her breath caught in her throat at the sight that greeted her. Thousands of tiny lights were strung from poles until they created a canopy of stars. Torches threw wavering light against the building, and as Tess looked more closely she realized that Drew had used the King Kamanimani South Seas Tiki Palace as inspiration.

She slowly moved toward the dinner table which had been set for two beneath the twinkling lights. Fresh flowers, heavily scented, were scattered over the table and she smiled at the coconut-shell glasses and bamboo place mats.

Something wet nudged at her leg and Tess cried out, then noticed Rufus standing beside her. He wore a glittering rhinestone collar and held a rose between his teeth. He laid the flower at Tess's feet, then trotted to the table and crawled underneath, circling once before settling himself with a soft "woof."

"I wasn't sure you'd come. Rufus was sure that you would."

Tess turned at the sound of his voice and watched as Drew appeared from the shadows. Her pulse quickened and she felt suddenly breathless. He was dressed in a tuxedo, exactly the way he was on the night they'd met. Tess swallowed hard, wondering if she'd be able to talk at all, unsure of what to say. "This is all so—so nice." She forced a smile. "And it doesn't even smell."

He stepped over to the table and held out a chair for her. Should she sit down or should she say what she came to say then leave? Tess hesitated. At that moment, she couldn't remember what she'd planned to tell him. All the words had fled her brain. And with her knees wobbling the way they were, it might be safer to get off her feet before she keeled over.

After he'd seated her at the table, Drew took his place across from her. As if on cue, soft music began to play and a waitress in a grass skirt appeared with a bottle of champagne. She poured it into the coconut shells, before slipping back into the shadows.

Tess squinted after her. "Isn't that the same waitress who—"

"I hired her for the night," Drew said. "I wanted everything to be perfect. Besides, King Kamanimani can do without her for an evening."

"I—I can't believe you did this," Tess murmured. "The alley looks like a fairyland. Nothing like the night we met."

Drew nodded. "Remember that night? The crab claws?"

"The dance," Tess added.

"The flat tires."

Tess squirmed in her chair. Why did he have to bring that up? Was he fishing for an apology? Or did he mean to remind her of all that had gone wrong between them. The flat tires had just been the start of their troubles.

"It looks just like the Tiki Palace," she said.

"Remember the pupu platter?" Drew asked. "I've never seen anyone eat so much, so fast."

"I didn't know what to say to you, so I ate. I had such a stomachache when I got home."

"I think you were just relieved that we didn't run into Lucy at Bistro Boulet. Elliot told me all about that night. I can imagine what you were thinking."

Tess glanced down, a soft sigh slipping from her lips. Why couldn't he leave it alone? Had he brought her here to torment her? How many more bad memories did he intend to dredge up?

As if he could read her mind, Drew reached out and took her hand. "Tess, look at what I've done here. Don't you understand what I'm trying to say?"

"You're trying to remind me of all the bad things that I did. The big mess I made of everything. And the big mess *you* made on top of my mess."

"But these aren't all bad memories," Drew said. "They can't be bad memories because they're *our* memories." He glanced around. "This is what we shared, Tess. It was crazy and confusing and sometimes painful, but it's our history. Good or bad, we went through this time together. And I don't want to forget it, because it brought you to me."

"Then—then you don't hate me?" Tess asked, looking up into his eyes.

"Hate you? How could I hate you? You were trying to protect your sister. Everything you did, you did out of love. I was just too stupid to see that. Too selfish and too proud.''

"I didn't do everything out of love," Tess admitted. "Making you dig that hole, that was out of spite."

Drew chuckled. "I deserved that. Do you realize how scared I was? I was sure you were going to go to jail and there was nothing I could do about it."

"I could tell," Tess said, a smile curling her lips. "I had such a hard time keeping a straight face. And I could hear Lucy giggling in the background the whole time."

He wove his fingers through hers and met her gaze, his blue eyes searching hers, as if he was trying to see inside her soul. "There's only one other time when I've been that scared," he said. "And that's the moment I realized I might lose you."

Tess's heart twisted and she glanced down at their hands. She couldn't tell his fingers from hers. And the emotions that she saw in his eyes, the regret and the forgiveness, mirrored her own feelings. "I came here to say goodbye," she murmured. "But I'm not sure I can do that now."

Drew stood up and pulled her to her feet. "Then don't. Don't leave me, Tess. I can't stand the thought of living without you."

"But so much has happened. We can't just forget that—"

He pressed a finger to her mouth to silence her, then slowly traced her lips, bending nearer. "I don't want to forget any of this. In fact, I want to remember every single detail of our lives together, from the moment we met. And I want to make more memories just like these."

"Just like them?"

"Exactly like them," he said, drawing her into his

arms. "And there's one memory in particular that I want most of all."

"And what is that?"

"I want this night to be a new beginning for us. I want to start over, Tess. I don't want to forget about our past, but I want to start thinking about our future. Together."

Tess couldn't believe what she was hearing. She'd come here to say goodbye and now he was asking her to stay. He wanted a future with her, a future that she'd dreamed of since the day they'd met. A future that she thought had been crushed among all the lies and deceit, lost forever.

"Watching Elliot's wedding," Drew said, "I realized that I wanted a happily-ever-after. And my ever-after wouldn't be happy unless you were part of it. I love you, Tess."

Her heart filled with all the emotion she'd held back for so long. For a moment, she wasn't sure she could speak. But then the words came so easily, as if she'd meant to say them all along. "And I love you, Drew."

With a low laugh, he pulled her against his body and brought his mouth down on hers. His kiss erased any doubts that she might still have had. Nothing stood between them now. The past had become something to treasure, memories that only made her love him more.

When he finally pulled back, Tess looked up into his handsome face, a face that she would spend a lifetime learning. "We sure picked a strange way to fall in love, didn't we?"

"But think of the stories we can tell our grandchildren," Drew said.

Tess giggled and he picked her up and spun her around in his arms. Rufus tangled in his feet, barking and jumping playfully. "They'll never believe us," Tess cried.

"Never!" he shouted.

Drew kissed her again, holding her against his lean body, her feet still inches off the ground. As his lips molded to hers, Tess wondered if she'd ever touch the ground again. She'd found love in the strangest way, all wrapped up in reprisal and revenge. But as her mind drifted from the past to the future, to her life with Drew, and to the children they'd have together, Tess came to realize what she'd known all along.

True happiness was the sweetest revenge of all.

HARLEQUIN SUPERROMANCE®

...there's more to the story!

Superromance. A *big* satisfying read about unforgettable characters. Each month we offer *four* very different stories that range from family drama to adventure and mystery, from highly emotional stories to romantic comedies—and much more! Stories about people you'll believe in and care about. Stories too compelling to put down....

Our authors are among today's *best* romance writers. You'll find familiar names and talented newcomers. Many of them are award winners—and you'll see why!

If you want the biggest and best in romance fiction, you'll get it from Superromance!

Available wherever Harlequin books are sold.

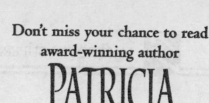

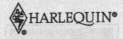

Not The Same Old Story!

 Exciting, glamorous romance stories that take readers around the world.

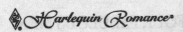 Sparkling, fresh and tender love stories that bring you pure romance.

 Bold and adventurous— Temptation is strong women, bad boys, great sex!

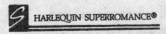 Provocative and realistic stories that celebrate life and love.

 Contemporary fairy tales—where anything is possible and where dreams come true.

 Heart-stopping, suspenseful adventures that combine the best of romance and mystery.

LOVE & LAUGHTER™ Humorous and romantic stories that capture the lighter side of love.

LOOK FOR OUR FOUR FABULOUS MEN!

Each month some of today's bestselling authors bring
four new fabulous men to Harlequin American Romance.
Whether they're rebel ranchers, millionaire power brokers
or sexy single dads, they're all gallant princes—and
they're all ready to sweep you into lighthearted fantasies
and contemporary fairy tales where anything is possible
and where all your dreams come true!

You don't even have to make a wish…
Harlequin American Romance will grant your every desire!

Look for Harlequin American Romance
wherever Harlequin books are sold!